THUNDER
Junior Park Ranger
IN ACADIA

Volume 2: Acadia National Park

Enjoy your National Parks!

Thunder

Trish Madell

Trish Madell

Dedicated to Feco, the first United States Coast Guard MSST Vizsla, and the coolest dog we've ever seen.

CHAPTER 1

I knew who I was, but I knew that he knew I wasn't who they thought I was. Yet so far, he hadn't said a word; he was just taking in information, assessing the situation. That's the thing about Labrador Retrievers—they're very chill. Of course, he had eyed me suspiciously when I first arrived, stepping shakily out of the Coast Guard van in front of the Southwest Harbor station. Now we were waiting in a staging area for deployment—whatever that means. The two humans waiting with us said they were going for coffee and walked out of the room, leaving the Lab and me alone. As soon as the door closed behind them, he looked me dead in the eye.

"Who are you," he demanded, "and where is Bomb Detection Canine Cooper?"

"I'm Thunder," I said nervously. "I'm a junior park ranger. Cooper is my neighbor, and he's probably with my partner, Ranger Mike, right now." He looked apprehensive, so I tried to explain. "It's a funny story, really. I mean, you know how humans are—they can't see a thing with their noses." I laughed uneasily. He didn't look amused;

he just continued to stare at me with those calm, unwavering eyes.

I had met Cooper back at the beginning of the summer. Ranger Mike and I had been assigned to Acadia National Park, and we had just arrived in Bar Harbor. We found our new quarters and worked diligently all day to unload the many boxes we had used to pack all of our clothes, dishes, leashes, toys, and everything else that had been in our old house. Late that afternoon, when the big moving truck was empty, Ranger Mike said to me, "Let's take a break, Thunder, and check out our new neighborhood."

Our house was near the end of a quiet street a few blocks west of the village green. I really liked our new house because it was close to the park, and the back yard led right into the woods, so there were lots of animals around. We saw a deer and some turkeys on that very first walk.

As we were heading back to our house, I saw another dog on a leash walking toward us. He was kind of funny looking: a skinny fellow with huge paws; big, dangly ears; and a rusty red coat. There was something odd about those gangly legs of his, like he had an extra set of knees or something, but he sauntered along with a stride as confidently fluid as a waterfall in spring.

I remember thinking that guy looked kind of familiar. I squinted my eyes to get a better look, and I saw he was taking a good, hard look at me too. We kept staring and walking toward each other until finally we met, eyeball to eyeball and nose to nose, or should I say big pink nose to big pink nose. *No wonder he looks familiar! He looks just like me!*

"Hey, dude," he barked, "are you a Vizsla?"

"Yeah, I'm a Vizsla. Are you a Vizsla?"

"Yeah, I'm a Vizsla," he answered. "My name's Cooper. I live in that house right there."

"You're kidding!" I said. "We just moved in right across the street. I'm Thunder. I'm a junior park ranger at Acadia National Park." After we gave each other a good sniff, I added, "We look a lot alike, you know. We could be twins."

"You're probably my doppelganger," Cooper observed.

"Hey, watch it," I said. "My mama told me not to talk like that. Besides, if anyone is anybody's doppelganger, you're my doppelganger."

"Don't get excited, buddy; it's not a bad word," Cooper explained. "It just means we're identical strangers. They say everyone has a doppelganger in the world somewhere, but not everyone gets to meet their doppelganger. That makes us pretty lucky."

"That makes sense. I am pretty lucky."

"Hey, I could show you around if you want since you're new on the island," he offered. "Meet you back here tonight?"

"Yeah, okay," I agreed. "See you after dinner.

* * *

I met Cooper outside, and we headed down to the waterfront. "Look, the tide is going out," he said, pointing across the bay. "We can go across to Bar Island. It's a fun place to explore."

We trotted up to where Bridge Street meets the Atlantic shore and then out onto the big sand bar that inspired the town's name. It was a great place to sniff. I scooped up a few of the lavender shelled muscles in my mouth. Mmmm, crunchy, just like potato chips. We explored the island shoreline until the sand gave way to slippery rocks covered with seaweed, and then we turned inland.

We followed the trail all the way to the far side of the island, where we found a mass of gulls enjoying a shore dinner on the rocky beach. "Come on. Let's scatter those gulls," Cooper suggested, and we took off at full speed, barking loudly as we ran. The startled gulls flapped into the air with their big gray wings. They circled above us for a moment, curious about what had disturbed their meal. When they saw it was us, they squawked loudly, giving Cooper and me a real chewing out.

One gull must have been particularly irritated. He swooped in, landing on a nearby boulder to give us a piece of his mind. "Just exactly what do you think you're doing? Can't you see we're trying to enjoy a nice meal at this lovely seaside eatery? Then you two hoodlums come along and scare the tail feathers right off of my rear. I use those feathers to steer, you know. Waak! Somebody! Check my butt!" he squawked.

"I'm terribly sorry, Gull. We were just having a little fun. We didn't mean to cause you any trouble," I offered sincerely.

"Yeah, me too. Sorry, Gull. We were just playing," Cooper added sheepishly.

"If it helps, your tail looks fine to me, and I don't see any extra feathers lying around here on the ground," I said reassuringly.

"So now you're a feather expert," he said sarcastically. "Thank you, Doctor Dog, but excuse me if I don't consider you and your furry friend, the best authorities on feather function. Look here."

He held out his right wing, exposing a small gap in the neat row of gray and white feathers. "I'm already missing F13. Those things don't grow back overnight you know."

We nodded.

"Do you even know what it takes to fly?"

"Um, no." We shook our heads.

"You have to be able to outsmart gravity," he said with a smug nod of his white feathered head. "For your information, it's gravity that's holding you down there on the ground right now, and it's gravity that keeps the air I fly through attached to the earth."

"But gravity acts on everything," I pointed out. "It must affect gulls too. Right?"

"Right, but I use gravity to fly because gravity causes air pressure, and that's the key to the whole thing," he said, pausing for effect as he folded his wing. "I use air pressure to get lift, and I use lift to fly."

"Lift?"

"You see, the pressure of the air that flows over your wings is lower than the pressure of the air that flows under your wings. If you go fast enough, the higher air pressure under your wings lifts you off the ground. That's why it's called lift."

I was skeptical, but on the other hand, the gull seemed to know what he was talking about, and he could fly. I pressed the issue. "It seems like air pressure would be the same everywhere. It's the same air, right?"

"Right, but because of the way a wing is curved, it has more surface area on the top than on the bottom, so air has to flow faster to get over the top of a wing. The faster the air flows, the less pressure it can exert," he explained. "If the wind is blowing just right, you hardly have to flap your wings at all. You just spread them out and expose the surface area." He tilted his head to the side and looked down his beak at us. "Now, can you two guess what makes up all that surface area on a bird's wing?"

"Feathers?" we responded in unison.

"Exactly."

"Oh!" Cooper interjected. "It's like how helicopter blades spin to make more air pressure underneath—so the helicopter lifts up."

"That's right," said the bird, a little surprised.

"Hey, how did you know that?" I asked Cooper, but before he could answer, all the other gulls in the group flapped their wings and flew out over the water in the direction of Bar Harbor.

"Where are they going so suddenly?" Cooper asked.

"We're done fishing here for tonight," the gull answered. "The tide's in."

"Wait! The tide is coming in right now, not going out?" Cooper shrilled with alarm. I, on the other hand, having almost no experience with tides either coming or going, had no idea why he might be concerned.

"That's right, pooch. The tide's coming in. G'night, boys. Enjoy spending the night on Bar Island," the gull chirped jovially as he flapped off in pursuit of his fellows.

"What's he mean by–" I began, but Cooper interrupted me.

"This is bad, Thunder! Come on. We've got to hurry!" Cooper took off at full speed and ran back toward the sand bar that formed a land bridge between Mount Desert Island and the much smaller Bar Island. I still didn't understand what the big emergency was, but I never really need a reason to hurry. If someone tells me to go fast, I'm automatically all in. I took off after Cooper and had almost caught up with him by the time he skidded to a stop at the sand bar, or rather at the place where the sand bar used to be.

CHAPTER 2

"What's going on?" I exclaimed. "What happened to the sandbar?" But even as I barked the words, I realized what had happened. On my last park assignment, in Vicksburg, Mississippi, there had been a huge flood that had displaced hundreds of animals. One of them was a king snake who had become lost when a sandbar in the river was completely submerged by the floodwaters. "Oh, I get it. The sandbar is underwater now, right?"

"Right," Cooper confirmed. "The tide has come in."

"So when the tide comes in, it means the water level goes up?"

"That's right," Cooper acknowledged. "We say the tide comes in or out because that's what it looks like on the beach or on the shoreline. High tide covers a lot of the rocks and beaches, while low tide leaves them exposed."

"And in this case, high tide covers the whole sandbar," I observed, "but for how long?"

"About six hours, dude."

"Six hours! Come on. It's not that far. Let's swim over," I suggested. "I don't want to be stuck here all night. Ranger Mike might think I'm lost."

"You first," he cajoled.

I stepped up to the edge of the water and looked back over my shoulder at Cooper. "I'm going. Are you coming?" I asked.

"Right behind you," he responded, nodding, but I noticed he didn't actually move.

"Here goes," I said, and I plunged into the water. The next thing I remember was loud splashing and shrill, high-pitched barking: "Ar! Ar! Ar! Ar!" It wasn't until I had managed to turn around in the water and scramble back onto the rocks that I realized it was me making all the noise.

"That's not like the water we have in Texas!" I coughed through my vibrating lips, giving myself a shake to dislodge as much of the frigid water as I could from the short, smooth hair that made up my coat. "Is it always that cold?"

"Ummmmm," Cooper pondered, looking for just the right words to explain the intemperate nature of the bright and oh-so-inviting-looking, crystal-clear water. "Yes," he finally conceded.

"Awesome," I said. "Hashtag I love camping!"

"Now you're talking!" he agreed, and we set

up a small campsite for ourselves behind some big boulders to block the wind. We turned a few circles to get oriented and said good night. I curled myself up tightly and tucked my nose under my arm to stay warm. I was asleep in no time.

We were awakened a few hours later by the same batch of gulls shrieking overhead. The tide had turned, and they were headed back to the beach for a breakfast of clams and cherrystone crabs, easily plucked from the newly exposed wet sand. "I've got to get home before Ranger Mike wakes up and misses me," I said. "I wouldn't want him to worry about me already. We just got here."

"Right behind you," Cooper said, only this time he jumped up to make good on his words. We were back to the neighborhood in a few minutes, and after a quick paw bump, we trotted up our opposing driveways to get ready for work.

Half an hour later, Ranger Mike and I hopped into our patrol truck and headed to the town pier for our first assignment as interpreters on the whale watch cruise. Captain Angie of the Friendship V met us at the gangplank to give us a tour of the boat.

"We keep life jackets in here, first aid supplies

are in this cupboard, and the restrooms are in the stern," she said, walking briskly along the aisle toward the stairs leading to the upper deck.

"What's in this big cupboard?" Ranger Mike asked, indicating a large cabinet marked HIGH SEAS EMERGENCY SUPPLIES.

"Oh, that's where we keep the barf bags," she explained while opening the door. We peered inside. The cupboard was stocked with bundles of white paper bags clearly marked with a red cross on the front. I could see there were several bundles and that each bundle held about a hundred bags. I'm not great with math, but I knew that added up to a lot of barf bags. Captain Angie called out to one of the deck hands, "Better stock the barf bags, Dylan. We're running low."

Ranger Mike and I looked at each other. "Running low?" he mouthed. I shrugged, and we moved on as we followed Captain Angie to the upper deck.

She indicated a platform in the bow. "This is where you can stand to interpret findings during the tour. The sound system is set up so that everyone on board can hear, even those inside and on the lower decks. To have a good chance of viewing whales, we travel out about fifteen or twenty miles to where the whales like to feed. It takes about an hour to get there, but there's plenty to see along the way." She turned to climb the ladder that led to the pilot house. "I've got to call the harbor master now. You two just make yourselves at home."

Ranger Mike and I started down the stairs to the lower decks. Captain Angie called after us, "Oh, by the way, I got a revised forecast this morning. It may be a little choppier than anticipated this afternoon. Could make for an interesting trip."

Ranger Mike and I looked at each other a moment, not sure how concerned we should be. The oceangoing part of this assignment was still pretty new to us, and we were learning the ropes as we went along. We didn't have much time to dwell on it though; passengers were beginning to come on board, so we turned to greet them, forgetting about the forecast for the time being.

"Welcome aboard," said Ranger Mike. "Find a place to sit for the trip out to the whale grounds."

I enjoyed all the attention I was getting while I waited to greet the canine guests.

"Oh, what a cute doggy!" a little girl with bright pink sneakers and a blond ponytail said as she stepped onto the deck. I put out my paw to shake her hand. She grasped it with enthusiasm and patted me on the head with her other hand.

When she let go of my paw, it was sticky. I sniffed. Mmmm, peanut butter and jelly! I licked my paw to remove the sticky mess. I mean, I had to, right? I couldn't greet the other guests with sticky paws.

A labradoodle with curly yellow hair was approaching with his family. "Welcome aboard," I said.

"Thank you," he responded, and then he added, "you have some peanut butter and jelly on your head."

"Yes, I know," I said. "Look out for the kid in the pink shoes."

"Right." He nodded.

Behind the doodle, a little girl with dark brown pigtails clasped in shiny yellow barrettes came aboard holding her daddy's hand. "Dad, look! A ranger dog!" she squealed, and they stopped to greet me. "What a sweet puppy," she went on as she threw her arms around me and gave me a big hug. I usually try not to while I'm on duty, but I couldn't resist. I reached out and gave her a little kiss. She giggled and said, "He likes me, Dad!"

Ranger Mike and I continued to greet guests as the boat filled up. Near the end of the line, a statuesque Great Dane walked regally up the ramp. She had a nice smile, a mostly white coat with a few splotches of black, and just a dusting of black freckles on her muzzle.

"Welcome aboard," I said. "I'm Thunder. I'm a junior park ranger, and I'll be your canine guide on the whale watch tour."

"Oh, how wonderful! I wasn't expecting a canine guide!" the Great Dane exclaimed. "My name is Marilyn. I'm on vacation with my family, and I'm really excited to see some whales!" Despite her regal appearance, her friendly demeanor made her seem very down to earth.

"You've come to the right place, Marilyn. We have several species of whales in this area of the North Atlantic. Minke, finback, pilot, humpback, and the extremely endangered right whales all spend the summer feeding off the coast of Maine." Overhead, the captain broadcast her safety announcement, and the boat began to back away from the pier. "It will take a little while to get out to the whale grounds, so make yourself comfortable."

I began the tour as we approached Egg Rock. "This small rocky island is called Egg Rock," I said to Marilyn and the doodle. "The island and the old lighthouse it holds mark the entrance to Frenchman Bay."

As the boat passed by the island, Marilyn

began barking loudly. "Ranger! Stop the boat! Stop the boat! There's a dog in the water!"

I rushed to the rail where she was standing. A harbor seal, with a slightly amu sed look on his face, was bobbing in the water below.

"It's okay, Marilyn," I explained. "He's not a dog. He's a sea dog—a harbor seal. Seals like to hang out around Egg Rock because the fishing is good and there's plenty of room to haul out of the water and sunbathe on the rocks."

"A sea dog! Well, they do look a lot like us!" Marilyn exclaimed. "They have a long muzzle and whiskers just like we do."

"Right. Seals are closely related to dogs. They even have sharp, pointy canine teeth like we have."

"I don't see any ears...can they hear?" the doodle asked.

"They have internal ears, so they can hear just fine," I answered. To demonstrate, I hollered out to the seal, "Good morning, seal. Whale watch coming through."

"Now see here, Ranger!" he bristled. "It's going to be a bit choppy out here this afternoon. I hope someone has stocked the barf bags on that bucket! The last thing I need is a boatload of queasy landlubbers upchucking fish food all the way back to the harbor. Some of us live in this water you know!"

"Uh, yes sir. Thank you. I'll take care of it," I said, smiling and nodding. *I wonder what he means by fish food. We don't let our guests throw anything into the water, especially not fish food.*

We continued out of Frenchman Bay and into open water. Soon, all around the horizon, nothing was visible but water in every direction. I already knew that the ocean was immense, everyone knows that, but there's a difference between knowing something because you have learned it and knowing something because you have seen it. You really have to see the open ocean to get an idea of how big it actually is—and just how big the planet we live on is to hold not only this ocean but another ocean and all the land in between. It really is amazing when you think about it. This is usually about where my philosophical reflection turns into a nap, but luckily, Marilyn spoke up with a question.

"Thunder, why did you call right whales *extremely* endangered?"

"Good question, Marilyn. I'm sure you know there are a lot of endangered species, and many of them are tagged and monitored in national parks.

But there are fewer than five hundred right whales left in the North Atlantic."

"Five hundred! What happened to them?"

"The problem goes back a long time, you see, before people knew much about conservation. Whale hunting used to be common, and some species of whales were hunted almost to extinction. Right whales and humpback whales were most vulnerable to whalers because they feed in shallower water. That's where the food they eat is found. It's illegal to hunt whales now, and that's helped a lot, but whales can get caught in fishing gear, they get hit by cruise ships and other boats, and oil spills and pollution kill the tiny crustaceans they eat. All of these other dangers make it hard for them to recover."

"Spout!" someone hollered, and I could feel the boat slowing to a stop. Human and canine passengers surged to the rail as they scanned the horizon for any sign of whales.

"Look! There's one!" I barked. Calling the canine passengers over to the rail, I pointed to what looked like water splashing a hundred yards ahead. The whale must have seen the boat too because it flipped its tail and disappeared under the water. I peered intently ahead as I tried to catch another glimpse of the magnificent creature.

I had always heard that humpback whales were big, happy clowns who loved to entertain, so I was surprised when this one disappeared so quickly. "Maybe it will surface again," I told my anxious charges. The three of us stood at the rail intently scanning the horizon for any sign of a water spout or a fin.

"Um, Hello-oh!" a giggly voice practically sang out. I looked around. "Down here! Duh, in the water!" We peered over the rail. Directly below us, a huge, rather pointy black and white face smiled up at us.

CHAPTER 3

"Hi! I'm Piper!" the whale said in a voice fairly bursting with enthusiasm. "Isn't this exciting? The first whale watch cruise of the season! It's so fun to see all the people riding out in boats to look at us! People are so interesting, don't you think? And dogs. Dogs are interesting too of course. I wouldn't want to give you the impression that I wasn't interested in dogs, because I am. I'm interested in everything, I guess. Aren't you? But of course you are—otherwise, why would you be on a whale watch cruise? Especially you, ranger. Park rangers have to take an interest in lots of different things because there are lots of different parks, right? I've visited some national parks. Acadia, of course," she giggled, "and Biscayne, Everglades, Dry Tortugas.... We always stop in for a quick visit whenever we are migrating past a national park. Dry Tortugas—that's a funny name for a park on the ocean, isn't it?"

"Uh, yes," I started to say, but Piper was already talking again.

"Oh, I'm sorry. I just, like, didn't even give

you a chance to introduce yourself. My bad. I'm just really so excited to meet you, especially since we're going to be working together on the whale watch tour. It's my first year on the entertainment committee, and I'm just, like, really excited. I just love people watching." She giggled. "There I go again, like, running my mouth at full speed. Right? Oh well, like I said, I'm excited. Now, you were saying..."

She paused for a moment and peered up at me inquisitively. I took that as my cue. "I'm Thunder, junior park ranger at Acadia, and these are my guests today."

"It's, like, so nice to meet you! I'm Piper! LOL, I forgot I already said that. Hey, did you get a good look at my fluke? Mine is mostly black with a little white patch. I'm just saying, because that's how you can tell it's me. The white patch is kind of shaped like a musical note, you know, with a little flag. That's why they call me Piper. See?" She dove under and lobbed the surface with her tail so we could get a good look, and sure enough, the white patches on her fluke resembled a quarter note with an oval and a flag.

"It does look like a musical note," I said when her face reappeared. "It's a beautiful name."

"Thank you, Thunder! You're so sweet!"

She giggled. "Anyway, that's how you can tell me apart from all the other humpbacks. That's how all whales are identified, mostly from the pattern on our flukes but sometimes from the shape of our dorsal fin or from scars. Most whales have scars. I'm missing the tip of my dorsal fin...lost it when I was a calf." She showed us her dorsal fin. "But it's, like, hard to see from a long way. It's much easier to see my tail."

I liked Piper already. She was so friendly and happy, and her enthusiasm was infectious. Sure, she had a musical note on her tail, but judging by the way our conversation had gone so far, I was not sure that was the only reason she had earned the name Piper. Words flowed so quickly out of her mouth that it seemed to me like they all came out at once. All I could really do was smile and nod as I attempted to follow along, and I was still trying to catch up when she said, "Hey, watch this!"

She slipped under the water and dove deep enough that we couldn't see her anymore. Everyone watched the surface with anticipation, including me. Since I had little experience with whales, I had no idea what to expect, but I certainly never expected what happened next. Piper burst through the surface of the water, flying high enough into the air that her whole enormous body hung over

the surface for an instant. Then, splashing down with such force, droplets of seawater fell on the boat like confetti. I barked my amazement, and all around me I heard exclamations of "Whoa!" from the people on board. Everyone was laughing, cheering, or barking.

"That move is called a breach. Did you like it?" she asked excitedly when her face popped back out of the water.

"Fabulous!" I barked. "Incredible!"

"Thanks!" She giggled. "There's more! Wait here. I'll be right back." She executed a quick turn and disappeared under the water, returning a few minutes later with another humpback beside her. "This is my BFF, Pearl."

"Hi," Pearl said shyly.

"We've been working on a special routine to, like, entertain people on the whale watch boats. We call it synchronized breaching. Watch!" Piper counted, "Ready! Five, six, seven, eight." Both whales dipped below the surface, a moment later springing out of the water together. Each whale holding her left flipper up and her right flipper down, they splashed back into the water on their left sides. Moments later the pair burst out of the water again, this time holding the right flipper up and splashing down on their right sides. It was amazing, but the whales were not finished yet. They swam in a circle around the boat, slapping their left fins on the water then rolling on their backs, executing a right fin slap, and then rolling dorsal fin up, kind of like a corkscrew pattern. After a couple of circuits, they arced gracefully beneath the surface, their dorsal fins and flukes disappearing at precisely the same instant.

"What a performance!" I howled when they came back up as everyone on board barked and cheered loudly. When the applause died down, my canine passengers joined their families to take pictures and watch for more whales, which gave me the opportunity to get to know the girls a little better.

"That routine was beyond amazing," I said sincerely. "You girls will be the stars of the whale watch."

"Aw, thanks, Thunder. We worked really hard on it," Piper said, grinning. "We've been working on it, like, ever since we left the West Indies."

"Wow, you swam all the way up here from the Caribbean! Aren't you two kind of young to be making a long trip like that?"

Both whales giggled. "No, silly," Piper explained, "we've been making that swim since we were calves and our moms brought us up here to spend the summer. We make that same trip every year because there's plenty of food here in the summer. You know, we eat a ton of food every day."

"Me too," I said. "I love kibble. I eat a ton of it!"

"Hahaha," the girls laughed.

"No, we're serious, Thunder. We literally eat a ton of food a day, mostly, like, krill and tiny fish. We gulp down seawater and filter the food out through the baleen in our throat. It's here, see?" Piper flipped on her back and swam a few meters, exposing the vertical lines under her chin. "We eat hearty all summer. Then, when it starts to get cold, we head back down to warmer waters in the Caribbean to spend the winter."

"It's the mating grounds," Pearl supplied, giggling and splashing water on Piper with her long pectoral fin.

"It is," Piper giggled, "but we're too young to pick a mate," she said as she splashed Pearl back.

"Piper likes Bosun," Pearl teased in a singsong voice.

"Do not." Piper giggled.

"Do too."

"Do not."

"Do too," Pearl said, and then, to be sure she got in the last word, she flipped herself underwater and lobbed the surface with her tail to make an extra splash.

"She's just kidding." Piper giggled.

"Her fluke is almost completely white," I observed. "That must be why she's called Pearl."

"Right! You're catching on, Thunder."

"And your dorsal fin...how did you lose the tip of your fin, Piper?"

"It happened when I was a young calf on my very first migration. Naturally, I was swimming with my mom, but I was, like, getting more adventurous, even though my mom kept telling me to stay close to her side. One day I saw these, like, pretty-colored things floating on the surface. I had never seen anything like that before, so I swam over to get a closer look. It was a bright sunny day, and dozens of the pretty-colored things sparkled on the surface with the sunlight behind them. They were marvelous. I was mesmerized by the colored light filtering through the clear water. I opened my mouth and took in a big gulp of seawater as I swam forward. I was delighted to be feeding in the colored wonderland, until I felt something strange in my mouth. That's when I noticed the lines of rope drifting down from the colored spots on the surface. I tried to spit the line out of my mouth, but I couldn't because it was attached to a heavy weight somewhere down below me. I was, like, surrounded by the long, colored lines. I tried to swim away from them, but the one stuck in my mouth got all tangled up with the others and somehow got wrapped around my flipper. I was terrified. I started to panic, swishing and flipping every part of me that I could still move, just trying to get away. Then, all at once, my mom was there in front of me. She gave me a nudge backward that freed the line from my mouth and my flipper. She pointed with her flipper. 'Swim that way! Now! Kick your fluke as hard as you can,' she said. I did what she told me, propelling myself forward as fast as I could. I could feel ropes brushing along my back and my flippers as I swam out of the nylon forest. I was almost clear when I felt something tightening around my dorsal fin. My heart sank. I couldn't move. I tried to keep kicking, but I started to cry. I couldn't help it; I was so frightened. I thought I was going to drown! I felt Mom nudging me, encouraging me to fight, so I kicked my tail as hard as I could. Something snapped, and I shot forward. I was finally in the clear, with no more lines around me. I looked back and saw Mom fighting her way through the tangled lines. She dodged and rolled her flippers out of the lines before they could tighten. Mom had migrated through enchanted forests of rainbow-colored lines and bobbers many times. She knew she would only have one chance to escape before the weight of the metal trap pulled the lines tight around her. Expending every ounce of strength in her ten-ton body, she breached high out of the water, using the weight of the trap to fling the wadded web of nylon off."

"Wow, I don't know what to say, Piper. I'm glad you both escaped. That must have been awful!"

"Oh, it was," Piper agreed, nodding her head emphatically, but then her face took on a thoughtful expression. "Terrifying...but it was also baffling. I just couldn't understand how something so beautiful could be so treacherous. It wasn't until after the ordeal was over and we were swimming away that I felt my dorsal fin throbbing, and I realized I had been injured." She paused for a moment and then giggled a little. "Mom calls it my lucky fin."

"It doesn't sound lucky." I cringed at the thought of how close Piper and her mother had come to disaster.

"Oh, we were very lucky that day, Thunder. Lots of whales get tangled up in fishing gear—even the biggest, strongest adult whales. Sometimes they can't get away at all, and sometimes they can still manage to swim and they drag the gear along with them for years. The lines are small, but they're very strong and hard to break. Mom and I could have drowned or starved to death. I could have lost her and been left on my own to figure out where to go and how to be a humpback whale. You better believe I stuck close to her side for the rest of that trip."

We heard the boat engines start, and Piper, bright and cheery once again, said, "That's my cue. I like to give the boat plenty of room to maneuver. I don't want any more lucky fins!"

"Right." I chuckled agreeably. "Bye, Piper. Thanks for the show, and tell Pearl I said thanks too."

"Bye, Thunder. See you on the whale watch!" she called.

We headed back toward Bar Harbor, and just as Captain Angie had predicted, the wind was blowing a little harder on the return trip, creating some bigger swells on the water. No one really noticed at first, but as the minutes ticked by, some of the passengers began to look a little less enthusiastic.

The two little girls who had greeted me so sweetly when they came aboard were sitting next to each other on the back row of the upper deck. One of them was clutching her tummy and whining in distress. I walked over and laid my head in her lap to comfort her. "Puppy," she said, "I don't feel good." Then she barfed all over my head.

Her mother saw the incident and jumped up to help. She took a couple of wobbly steps in our direction and then—splat! She threw up on me too. I could feel it running down the back of my neck— so gross! I shook my head, flapping my ears back and forth as I tried to get the barf off my neck, splattering everyone in the last four rows in the process.

"Break out the barf bags!" the captain ordered. "Hurry! Before it's too late!"

I looked around. Marilyn wavered unsteadily on her paws, the short white hair around her muzzle now backlit with a greenish hue. She made heaving noises as she stumbled toward the rail, where she collapsed, her paws splayed out on both sides, head hung over the side in puke position. Unfortunately, at just that moment, the boat tilted on a wave so that the huge dog's heroic effort not to hurl on those around her backfired on passengers standing portside on the second deck.

"Ew!" someone shrieked below.

I stood there momentarily stunned as the scene unfolded. Dylan was passing out barf bags while all around me I heard the echo of spew and splat. I scanned the deck for the doodle, hoping for a little backup. There he was, huddled under some empty seats by the stairwell. He had his head down, paws over his ears and eyes squeezed shut. I wished I'd thought of that.

"Get a mop and a bucket!" the captain hollered over the noise. "Emergency! All hands on deck."

Eventually, we made it back to Frenchman Bay. Some of the sick passengers were still draped over the rail like wet laundry as we passed Egg Rock. I saw the same harbor seal from this morning hauled out on the rocks, taking in the sun. He shook his flipper at me.

"The head ranger will hear about this," he hollered.

Great, I thought, *a complaint on my first day on the job. That's got to be some kind of record.*

When we got to the dock, the passengers filed off the boat like zombies. Ranger Mike and I drove home in complete silence. We pulled into the driveway, and he cut off the engine.

"Let us never speak of today's cruise again," Ranger Mike said solemnly, and I nodded.

* * *

CHAPTER 4

Our new house in Bar Harbor was missing one important thing: a junior ranger door. You know what I mean—one of those little doors cut into the bottom of the big door so dogs can go in or out whenever they want. I suppose that wouldn't be a big deal to some, but this afternoon it was a flaw of which I had become keenly aware. Ranger Mike had been gone for hours, and I had urgent business to attend to—really, really urgent business. For a while, I stood by the door waiting patiently for him to return so I could go outside. Now I was waiting not so patiently by the door, beads of sweat forming on my brow. I had begun to hum to distract myself from my predicament when Spot sauntered into the room.

"Whatcha doing?" she purred.

"I'm just waiting for Ranger Mike to get home," I answered.

"Why are you turning yourself inside out like that?" she cooed.

"I'm fine, thank you," I replied.

"Come on. You look positively miserable. Why not find yourself an out-of-the-way corner somewhere in the house?"

"I can wait, thank you," I said curtly.

"Oh, I'm sure you can. I'm sure you're just a whizzzz at waiting, aren't you? I'm sure Ranger Mike is urrrgently finishing up his business so he can rush right home to relieve you. It might take a while though; he's off the island. He'll have to pass by a lot of water along the way."

"Will you cut it out?" I pleaded impatiently. The pressure was beginning to get to me.

"Find an open closet. That's the ticket, buddy. Who'll ever know? Or better yet, drop it right there on the carpet. After all, it's not your fault, is it? You can't open the door, can you? So when you think about it, it's all Ranger Mike's fault. He's in charge, right? How could he blame you? It's almost like he's asking for it."

I was shocked. I gathered my dignity and looked her straight in the eye. "I am a pointer. I come from a long line of champion pointers who could point and flush game anytime, anywhere. No one in my family has ever gone in the house, and I am not going to be the first!"

"Sure thing, pal," she crooned with mock

sympathy. "Just one thing...as long as you're waiting up for Ranger Mike, can you tell him the faucet in the kitchen sink is leaking? Drip, drip, drip...that thing runs all the time. Of course, it's just a piddle, but every wee bit of water adds up, and next thing you know, there's a big puddle on the floor. Know what I mean?"

"Spot, pleeeeease give me a break here."

"You're welcome to use my sand box. I won't tell a soul. It'll be our little secret. I promise, cross my heart." A breeze blew past the wind chimes outside, and Spot put her paw up to her ear. "Hear that? Tinkle, tinkle, tinkle...such a pleasant sound. So relaxing, don't you think?" She was really laying it on thick while she had the chance, but finally, I heard the welcome sound of a vehicle approaching the house.

"Please be Ranger Mike, please be Ranger Mike," I mumbled, hoping out loud. By now I had both my front and hind legs tightly crossed. *Yes! I see headlights!* But they stopped at the mailbox. "Come on, come on," I whispered.

"Looks like you're in luck, buddy. You just might make it tonight," Spot said, taking the opportunity to get in one last dig. "I was just trying to help, you know."

I ignored her last remark as I danced back and forth from paw to paw as the headlights approached the house. I stared intently at the door, willing it to open.

"Hi, guys. Sorry I was gone so long," Ranger Mike called out as he walked through the door.

I rushed past him at full speed, almost knocking him off his feet. I dove off the porch and in a couple of galloping strides made it to the tree line, the premier potty spot in the yard. I didn't even sniff. I just lifted my leg and went for it. *Ahhhhhh. That's better!*

After that close call, Ranger Mike thought it was a good idea to install a junior ranger door right away. Assisting Ranger Mike with the project gave me an idea, and by the time we were finished, I had constructed a plan to get even with Spot for torturing me. My plan would require the help of my doppelganger from across the street, so I ambled over to recruit his assistance and to fill him in on my plan.

The next time Ranger Mike left for the evening, we were ready.

"Feel free to use the junior ranger door anytime you like, Spot," I said generously, stepping aside so she could go through.

"Thank you, but I don't need your permission," she snipped as she carefully nudged the door open with her nose and stepped through to the outside.

Cooper was stationed in the yard on the other side of the small door. "Come on out. It's a beautiful day," he said as soon as she stepped through and the door flapped shut.

Spot arched her back and jumped, all four paws leaving the ground simultaneously.

"How did you do that?" she demanded.

"Do what?" Cooper said innocently.

"How did you get out here so quickly? You were just inside!" She turned and re-entered the house through the flap.

I was waiting for her inside. "Nice day out there, isn't it?" I said sweetly.

She did a double take and then quickly stuck her head back outside. Cooper was out of sight, just as we had planned. She confronted me. "Okay, smarty pants, how are you doing that?"

"Doing what?"

"How are you in two places at one time?"

"I don't know what you're talking about, Spot. I'm just sitting here."

She turned and dove back through the junior ranger door.

Cooper was waiting with a smile on his face. "See, just sitting here." She darted back inside.

"That was fast," I teased. "Don't feel like playing outside?"

"No, I think I'll go lay down for a while," she meowed.

"That's probably just as well," I said. "I mean, there are a lot of dangers out there for a small cat like you. Eagles, falcons, and hawks would just love to swoop in and snatch up a tasty kitty. And the owls...don't get me started on the owls.

"Hoo...hoo...hoo" came from outside as Cooper provided his best impression of a barred owl.

"The other rangers say that barred owls just love to bring cats home for dinner." I could see we were starting to get to Spot, so I laid it on thick. "What's that?" I said, placing my paw by my ear and pretending to hear something else outside. "Coyotes? I think I hear a coyote out there. Do you hear a coyote, Spot?"

Right on cue, we heard, "Yowwwww, yip, yip, yowwwwwww," as Cooper impersonated a coyote.

"You're just trying to scare me." She turned

and flicked her tail at me. After a moment's hesitation, she pushed open the junior ranger door and caught Cooper in mid-yip. "Two of you!" She lifted a paw to her forehead. "I don't know why you're trying to scare me with all that talon talk and coyote yipping. Double the dog is already twice as terrifying." She backed through the door and disappeared into her evil basement lair as I nosed through the door flap to give Cooper a high five.

＊

CHAPTER 5

A few days later, Ranger Mike and I were assigned to trail maintenance on Champlain Mountain. We had a short but picturesque commute to Hulls Cove along the eastern edge of the island. Ranger Mike stopped in at the general store for coffee and doughnuts, and he gave me the doughnut hole. *This day just keeps getting better. I really am a lucky dog.*

We would be working with the Summit Stewards today, a team of mostly college students employed for the summer season. I always enjoyed meeting volunteers and summer staffers because I have noticed, during my tenure in the parks, that these groups are particularly prone to having dog biscuits in their pockets.

We were to meet the group at the parking lot of the Precipice trailhead. The Precipice is one of the most popular trails in the park and leads the very bravest hikers along narrow, exposed ledges up the sheer cliff face of Champlain Mountain. Despite its popularity, the trail is usually closed most of the spring and summer so that peregrine falcons nesting on the ledge are not disturbed by hikers. We arrived to find Ranger Bruce setting up a falcon watch station near the parking lot.

"Good morning, Ranger Bruce. I heard there was exciting news about this peregrine nest," Ranger Mike called out.

"Yes, indeed. Come have a look."

Ranger Mike leaned down to look through the telescope trained on the cliffside nursery. "You see, the falcons are tending to three hatchlings this year. This is the same pair of falcons that had a successful nest here last season. I think they have a good chance to get all three chicks fledged," Ranger Bruce explained.

I took the opportunity to check my messages. It was not that I was not interested in the falcons; of course I was. It's just that dogs aren't very good at looking through a telescope; there's nowhere to put our noses. So I sniffed around the bottom of the signpost to see if anyone had posted anything interesting.

A couple of corgis posted that they were having a great vacation. I liked it.

A rottweiler posted a complaint that there weren't enough extra-large poop bags in the dispenser. I liked it, and I gave him an LOL.

A bear posted instructions on how to bypass the latch on the trash cans. *Hey!* I scratched dirt all over that post. *That's not what this board is for. If bears can't follow the rules, then they can't post here.*

I saw the steward's van pull into the parking lot, and I trotted over to meet the group. I was greeted enthusiastically. No doubt they were pleased to learn they would have the help of an experienced junior ranger on today's crew. A young woman called Charlie pulled a big dog biscuit out of her pocket. "Who's a good boy?" she lilted. "Who's a very good boy?"

"I am!" I barked. "I'm a good boy!"

She gave me the biscuit, and I crunched it right down. With the introductions and formalities out of the way, Ranger Mike joined us, and we walked a short way up to the north face trailhead and started up the mountain, checking for blaze marks and official cairns as we walked.

A cairn is a stack of rocks that marks a trail. Two large flat rocks are placed side by side, with another on top. Then a smaller rock is placed on that to point the way. Cairns are traditional in Acadia, and they work very well here because a lot of the trails wind along over bare granite. There are plenty of rocks around, and sometimes visitors make their own cairns for fun. Those cairns may accidently cause hikers to get lost, so the stewards maintain the official cairns and get rid of the extras.

It was a glorious day to be outside. The view was amazing. From the trail, the conifer-covered Porcupine Islands looked like mossy green stepping stones placed in the water by a giant who didn't want to get his feet wet while wading across the bay. Personally, I was not familiar with that variety of pine—the pork-u-pine, I mean. I knew the red pine, white pine, and even the loblolly pine, but I'd never heard of a pork-u-pine. *No matter. I'm sure I'll come across one sooner or later,* I supposed.

Cairn maintenance and trail clearing were not our only duties. The summit stewards are also eager to inform visitors about the principles of park conservation. One of the most important is called 'leave no trace.' It's very simple. It means that no one who hikes along the trail after you should know you were ever there.

For instance, suppose you are hiking and you get tired and hungry. You stop for a rest and pull an apple out of your pocket, and your sister eats an orange she brought in her backpack. After your snack, there should be orange peel in her backpack and an apple core complete with seeds and stem in your pocket. And there should also be nothing in your pocket or her backpack that you didn't bring with you. Examine all the rocks, shells, and flowers you want, but don't take them with you. Leave them there for someone else to find.

At its best, leave no trace includes picking up any litter you find along the way. So naturally, when I saw a plastic cup in some blueberry bushes a short way off the trail, I walked over to pick it up. However, as I approached the cup, it moved away from me—all by itself. Baffled, I watched the cup slowly weave its way through the bushes and into a patch of the stubby pine trees, which were scattered here and there between expanses of bare rock. I followed the mysterious litter as it moved farther and farther from the trail. I wanted to pick it up, but every time I reached for the cup, it moved farther away. "Wait!" I called out in frustration, immediately laughing at myself for talking to a plastic cup.

But then the cup answered back. "Welp!"

I froze. Did I really hear that? Did that cup speak? "I beg your pardon?" I offered tentatively.

"Welp! Wy wed," it responded.

It's not every day that one is confronted

by talking litter; however, rules are rules, and littering is against the rules. "Wop!" I hollered. "I mean stop! Littering is against park rules!"

The cup stepped out into the open and turned to face me. Now I could see that it wasn't moving on its own but was attached to some kind of critter I had never seen before. Its face, its whole head really, was stuck inside the cup. *That's very odd? What kind of critter mumbles and carries a cup around on its head?*

Then suddenly I realized—"Oh! You need help! Don't worry. I'm a junior ranger. I can help you." I approached slowly, trying to speak in a calm, reassuring voice. "Here, I'll just pull that cup off your face, and you'll be good as new." I stretched out my neck to grab the cup with my mouth, the best grasping tool I had.

The critter took a small step back. "Wareful, wanger. I'm a workuwine," he said urgently, his voice still muffled by the cup.

"I'm sorry, sir, but I can't understand what you're saying. Just let me help you get that cup off your—"

I was interrupted again, this time by Charlie's urgent shout from the trail. "Thunder, look out! That's a porcupine!"

I looked over at Charlie and then up at the tree. It was a dwarf pitch pine, like most of the trees near the top of the mountain, but why was Charlie trying to give me a lesson in horticulture right now? "It's a pitch pine," I barked. "You can show me a pork-u-pine later, thank you." I smiled and nodded at Charlie before turning back to the distressed animal. "Now let me help you, sir."

This time I grasped the cup delicately in my mouth and gave a little tug. "Still stuck. Let me just get a little leverage." Still holding the cup, I put my front paws on the critter's shoulders and tugged. I fell back on my haunches as the cup popped right off, no problem. It was when I put my paws down to stand up that there was a problem. A big problem!

It felt as if my paws had spontaneously burst into flames. "Ar-ar-ar-ar-arrrrr," I yelped. There were dozens of long, sharp barbs poking out of my paw pads and some on top of my paws too. I felt my face burning and delicately touched my muzzle. "Owww." There were some in my face too. I tried to dislodge the needles by shaking my head as hard as I could, but that only made it worse and left me with a cut on my ear.

"I'm sorry, Ranger. I tried to warn you that I'm a porcupine," he said clearly now that the cup had been removed. "If it's any consolation, I really appreciate your help. I've been trying to get that cup off my head all morning." Charlie grabbed Ranger Mike, and the two hurried toward us. "Thanks again, ranger, got to go," the porcupine said and scurried off through the patch of trees and out of sight.

"Owwwww," I wailed pathetically.

"Aw, poor Thunder. That's a hard way to learn what a porcupine is," Charlie said sympathetically.

Ranger Mike just shook his head. "It's a carry out," he hollered. "We're going to need a stretcher up here."

The summit stewards brought a stretcher and helped me get on. With one on each corner, four of them carried me back down the mountain trail with Charlie walking along beside me.

Ranger Mike loaded me into our patrol truck and drove me straight to the veterinary clinic. Every time I moved my head, blood from the cut on my ear splattered the dashboard, windows, seats, and Ranger Mike. By the time we arrived, the truck looked like a crime scene.

At the clinic, I learned the sharp barbs lodged in my snout and paws were called quills. They easily transfer from the host to the victim;

just brushing against a porcupine will get you a nice batch of quills. The quills are also really hard to remove and keep working their way deeper into your skin the longer they stay. Nothing can be done except to pull out each quill one at a time.

"It's a new record," Ranger Mike said. "Emergency vet visit our first week on the job."

How was I supposed to know? I sat patiently as the doctor extracted the quills from my face and paws. "You're lucky," she said. "Some of my patients can't sit down."

Yikes! I didn't even want to think about that. Eventually, all the quills were gone, and she took a look at my ear. "That's going to need a stitch and some bandages," she announced as she performed the stitches so quickly that I hardly knew it was happening.

It's kind of hard to bandage floppy hound dog ears like mine, so she wrapped the soft gauze bandages all around my head to hold my ears in place. I felt kind of nice after my injury, soft and comforting. "There you go," she said, stepping back to admire her work with a big smile on her face.

The vet tech who had assisted her was smiling too, almost giggling really. *That's nice,* I thought. *This is a friendly place.* I smiled back warmly, and she patted me on the head. "You're a good patient, Thunder. Come on. Let's see if we can find you a dog biscuit." She giggled and pulled a treat out of her pocket.

I ate the treat in one bite. Rescuing dangerous animals takes a lot out of you. After all, that porcupine was in a terrible jam. He couldn't eat or drink with that cup on his head. He told me himself that he had tried to remove it but couldn't. I mean, I was kind of a hero when you think about it. Of course, I didn't want any fuss about that— you know, because I was injured and all. I was just a junior ranger doing my job.

I imagined the scene when Ranger Mike and I would return to park headquarters with me in bandages. The summit stewards would have already told the other rangers about my bravery and devotion to duty. When we walked in, they would all stand up, applauding and cheering. "It was nothing, nothing at all," I imagined myself saying. "I saw a creature in need and rushed to his aid without any thought for my own personal safety." They would all pet me, say, "Good boy, Thunder," and offer me treats. I might even be ranger of the month! With that scenario playing in my head, I dozed off for a short nap while I waited for Ranger Mike to pick me up.

In no time at all I heard the doctor call, "Ranger Mike is here." She opened the crate where I had been resting. "Come on, handsome," she said, leading me out to the waiting room.

As we walked in, Ranger Mike burst out laughing. "Hot pink!" he blurted out, pointing at me.

"Yes, sorry about that, Ranger Mike." The vet laughed. "His ear was still bleeding, and the only bandages we had on hand were hot pink."

Startled, I looked from Ranger Mike to the vet and back to Ranger Mike. *What are they talking about?* I wondered. I turned around in a circle, trying to get a better angle, but all I could see were my back legs and my butt with my still-wagging tail. Then I caught my reflection in the big glass window and my tail froze mid-wag. "Noooooooooo!" Bright pink bandages! I looked like such a dork! "Please, doctor, don't you have any bandages in hunter orange?" I whined. *I'm a hunting dog! I have my reputation to think about! What are the other rangers going to say?*

When we walked into the conference room at park headquarters half an hour later, the ranger meeting had already started, and the whole summit crew was there. There was applause, just like I had imagined, but it was accompanied by wild laughter. One ranger said, "Thunder, you could wear that outfit to the prom," and everyone laughed some more.

I walked over to the corner and flopped down by myself. I didn't even listen to the meeting; I just stared out the window and sulked. Was that any way to treat a hero and an injured hero, at that? I barely noticed when the meeting broke up and everyone left the room except Charlie. She came over to my corner and sat down beside me.

"I think you were very brave, Thunder. Most people would have been too afraid to help that poor porcupine, but you never hesitated. You're a good boy, Thunder, and a good ranger." She hugged me and pulled two more dog biscuits out of her pocket. My spirits lifted as I crunched into the cookies and gave her a big kiss.

CHAPTER 6

I spent the next few days at home recovering from my porcupine encounter, which gave me a chance to get to know the neighborhood a little better. It turned out Cooper and I were not the only canine neighbors of the same breed. My next-door neighbors on both sides were golden retrievers. But they weren't really doppelgangers. Actually, they don't look much alike at all.

Reggie, a distinguished elderly golden, lived with his family in the house on the right. He was rather frail and hard of hearing, but his mind was as sharp as a tack. He was well-respected, and of course, as the senior dog, he headed up the neighborhood security watch.

Next door on the other side was...well, on the other side was Ciara. I could see her out the window when she fetched the mail. Her thick, fluffy coat was the color of daffodils, and her big, round face was like sunshine. At eighty plus pounds, she was a substantial woman, solid on her paws as she lumbered down the driveway like a tank. *I might be in love*, I thought as I gazed at her through the window.

I would like to get to know her better, but how? I've been trying to get her to notice me all week. The other day, I saw her outside in the yard, so I ran in the house, grabbed my tennis ball, and told Ranger Mike that I had to play right away. Ranger Mike threw the ball for me a few times, and I made some spectacular catches— with my head still in bandages—but she barely even glanced in my direction.

So I decided that what I really needed was a good excuse to enter her yard. Once there, I could engage her in casual conversation, you know, to find out what she liked to do. Then I could suggest an outing together or something. It had to be a good excuse though. I mean, one dog can't just barge into another dog's yard; in terms of canine etiquette, it's considered terribly rude.

I glanced around the yard for ideas. Over in the back corner, I saw a sliver of red peeking out from under a bushy tuft of fountain grass. That was it! My old red Frisbee. I had gnawed on it so much that it wouldn't fly anymore. No problem—I didn't need it to fly. I would just drop it in Ciara's yard, and then, when she came outside, I would casually wander over looking for it. It would be the perfect ice breaker.

I picked up the dilapidated toy and made my way over to her yard. *Now, where can I stash it so that I can pretend to be looking for it later?* Along the side of the porch was a row of flowering lilac bushes that had potential as a casual hiding place. I carried the Frisbee over, but as soon as I got close, my nose began to tickle. "Ah–ah–ah–choo!" *Yikes! I forgot that lilacs make me sneeze. I better hurry.* I dropped the Frisbee and pushed it under the bush with my nose. "Ah–choo!"

"Woof" Ciara appeared on the front porch out of nowhere.

Uh oh, she must have heard me sneeze.

"Uh, good afternoon, Ciara. Lovely day."

"Yes, it is," she said politely. "May I help you with something, Thunder?"

"Um, yes." I hesitated nervously. My excuse now seemed trite and ridiculous. I mean, Ciara was a retriever; she was going to know that chewed up Frisbee wouldn't fly. But I couldn't think of anything else to say. "I–I was just looking for... for my red Frisbee." I could feel a simpering smile forming as my face chose to throw itself on the mercy of the court and to leave my brain to defend the flimsy excuse alone.

Amused, she nodded toward the toy. "If you

mean the one you just sneezed on, it's right there under your nose."

"Oh, yes, of course, here it is," I blathered. I could feel my cheeks flooding with color until I was sure they must be glowing as brightly as the hot pink bandages.

"Is there anything else I can help you find?" she inquired, her tone of voice giving me the impression that she hadn't been fooled at all by the Frisbee ploy.

"Uh…" *Think fast, Thunder.* "Uh, yes. Um, have you seen a white kitty around?"

"If you mean Ranger Mike's white cat," Ciara nodded, "she's right behind you."

I turned. Spot was sitting a few feet behind me witnessing the entire humiliating exchange. I turned back to Ciara. "Yes, that's her. Thank you." I smiled. "See you around, then, I guess."

She nodded, and I turned to Spot. "Come on," I said, walking back toward our yard.

"That was pathetic." Spot snickered.

***

A few days later, the bandages were off. I was ready to return to work with Ranger Mike, but

I still hadn't managed to get Ciara's attention.

"If you want to talk to her, catch her at the mailbox," Spot had suggested. "She fetches the mail every morning for her mom."

Taking Spot's advice, I ducked out the junior ranger door as soon as I saw the mailman and meandered around the porch until I saw Ciara trotting down her driveway toward the mailbox. Then I casually made my way to Ranger Mike's mailbox at the end of our driveway. "Good morning, Ciara! Beautiful day today!" I said, trying not to pant too loudly. "Are you going for a walk today? Huh, are you?"

"Oh, hi, Thunder. I don't know...maybe."

"We could walk over to Little Long Pond and go swimming! I know you like swimming!"

"Meh, I do like swimming. I don't know... maybe." She took the mail from the mailbox and loped back toward the house, the long guard hairs in her coat swaying back and forth in syncopated rhythm with her tail wag.

"Ahhhh," I sighed.

BEEEEEP! "Hey, are you coming to work today?" Ranger Mike barked from the rolled down window of the patrol truck. Startled, I jumped a bit. I never even heard the garage door open.

I hopped in the truck. "Just waiting on you," I yipped, but he didn't buy it.

While I was home recuperating, Ranger Mike and I had given a lot of thought to the problem of keeping canine visitors to Acadia safe while they were enjoying the park. We had come up with an idea that we would be presenting at this morning's ranger meeting.

"Part of the problem," Ranger Mike said, addressing the crowded conference room, "is that dogs come from all over to visit Acadia, so they may not be familiar with the animals and the terrain they encounter during their visit. Unfamiliar sights, sounds, and scents may distract calm, normally well-behaved dogs."

It was true that sights and sounds could be very distracting, but scents? Don't even get me started on how enticing unfamiliar scents can be! When I pick up a totally unfamiliar scent, it's like my nose takes over my whole body! It drags me right off the trail toward that scent, wherever or whatever it may be. You can see how that could be a problem, of course, particularly if the unfamiliar scent is, say, too close to the edge of a cliff or coming from a bear.

"The other part of the problem," Ranger Mike went on, "is that dogs may scare people or other animals in the park. Even very friendly dogs may accidently scare birds away from their nests or other animals away from sources of food and water."

The idea was immediately popular since almost every ranger in the room had been involved with some kind of pet predicament at some point in their career. It wasn't long before some of the rangers and stewards were contributing suggestions. "We could invite everyone who visits the park with their pets to a safety orientation," one of the rangers suggested. "We can teach them how to keep their pets safe and protect wildlife in the park."

"Dogs could earn a certificate when they pass the class or maybe a badge—something that distinguishes their conservation efforts," another ranger offered.

"Those are great ideas," Ranger Mike acknowledged, "but there's still one important issue to be discussed—poop. Specifically, dog poop." The crowd snickered a little, but Ranger Mike continued, "We can't avoid the dog poop, so there's no point trying to sidestep it." There was more laughter, a little louder this time. "I'm serious, people. If we can't get a handle on the poop, we might as well squash the whole thing."

"Ew!" somebody said loudly, and the whole room dissolved into laughter.

After a few moments, the head ranger said, "Okay, okay, everybody, Ranger Mike is trying to tell us about a serious poop problem!" After the last few snorts were stifled, he said, "Go ahead, Ranger Mike."

"Dog poop can contaminate drinking water and spread diseases to wildlife populations," Ranger Mike explained, "so poop must be bagged and the bags disposed of properly."

"Okay, I think we've got it," the head ranger said. "Do you have a name for the program, Ranger Mike? What are we going to call our safety-certified, four-legged park patrons?

"We don't have a name yet. Does anyone have a suggestion?" Ranger Mike asked the crowd.

Everyone was excited about the idea and began to brainstorm possible names.

"The Poop Patrol."

"The Baggie Brigade."

I raised my paw too, but Ranger Mike hadn't noticed me yet, so I barked to get his attention.

"Arf!"

"The Conservation Canine Corps."

"The Tail Crew."

"Arf! Arf!" I barked excitedly with my paw still in the air.

"Maintenance Mutts," someone called out from the back of the room.

Sitting next to me, Charlie saw me straining to get Ranger Mike's attention.

"Arf!" I barked. "Arf! Arf! Arf!

"What is it, Thunder?" she asked, studying my intense body language and urgent expression.

"Arf! Arf-arf!" I explained again, this time directly to Charlie.

A big smile spread across her face. "That's it, Thunder! The perfect name." She jumped to her feet. "We'll call them Bark Rangers!"

CHAPTER 7

"Okay," said the Labrador calmly, "so you and Canine Cooper are acquainted, but that doesn't explain why you're here at the Coast Guard Station, and he isn't."

"Well no...but I'm getting to that part," I stammered.

"Get to it then," he said. "I don't have all day."

"Okay, okay...well, Acadia is a busy park with a lot going on, and Ranger Mike and I had spent our first few weeks learning the particulars of the place you know. But now we were up to speed, and just in time too because we were coming up on the Fourth of July weekend—one of the biggest events of the season. The park was anticipating a lot of extra visitors as people flocked into Bar Harbor for the holiday. Ranger Mike and I were assigned to the information desk at the visitor center for the morning shift."

Now, the information desk is not the most glamorous job in the park, but that doesn't mean it's not important. The rangers at the desk tell visitors about points of interest along the tour road. They help locate campsites, plan hikes and bicycle routes, and answer questions about trails, beaches, and park rules. Manning the information desk means answering lots of questions. As a matter of fact, the assignment is a favorite of rangers who say they enjoy answering the same questions over and over all day long. Even so, there is one particular question that stands out from the rest in terms of frequency.

"Where are the rest rooms?"

"Just inside the visitor center to your right, ma'am," Ranger Mike answered politely.

I couldn't tell you exactly how many times a day we hear that question; I'm not great with numbers. Let's just say it's a lot. This time the question in question came from a woman in hiking boots, pushing a double decker baby stroller with a smiling toddler in front and a tiny baby sleeping in the back. Ranger Mike opened the door for her, and the toddler reached out to give me a quick pat, depositing a sticky substance on my face as the stroller swung past on its way to the facilities.

Mmmm...blueberry syrup! As an official park representative, I believe it is important to present a tidy appearance. So even though it took some tongue acrobatics, I managed to lick the syrup off my cheek and muzzle.

Next up was a couple with a brown and white curly haired terrier. The terrier had an urgent look on his face. "Poop bags!" he said. "I need poop bags!"

"Around the corner, buddy." I pointed. "You're headed in the right direction."

"Thanks," he called back over his shoulder as he led his human companions around to the canine rest area.

We try to be prepared, but some questions are just impossible to anticipate.

"Good morning, ranger. How tall do you have to be to ride the roller coaster?"

"What roller coaster?" Ranger Mike asked.

"Oh, any of them. How many do you have at this park?"

"We don't have any roller coasters. It's not that kind of park."

"What do you mean it's not that kind of park? What kind of park is it?"

"It's the kind of park where you get to enjoy the unspoiled beauty of nature."

"Nature, huh? But what about the kids? How

will we entertain them? They are used to a lot of excitement from video games and thrill rides."

"Don't worry. Kids find nature very entertaining," Ranger Mike assured him, handing him information about ranger talks and the nature cruise and then helping him locate their campsite on the map.

I don't want to give you the wrong idea. It's not all about poop bags and such. I get the opportunity to meet lots of great dogs, some really cool people, and occasionally even a cat that's not too obnoxious. Like the two German shepherds who stopped by the visitor center this morning— they introduced themselves as Finn and Oskar. They explained that they belonged to a search and rescue team based in Pennsylvania and that they were on vacation with their human partners this week.

"Search and rescue! That sounds like exciting work," I said.

"Yes, it can be," Finn said. "We closed a case a few days ago, as a matter of fact, that was very intense. A little boy about two years old wandered out of his yard while his dad was mowing the lawn. Even though it had only been a few minutes, his parents couldn't find him anywhere. All the neighbors joined in the search, but it was starting to get dark, so they called the police. K-9 Officer Rusty responded right away with a couple of human officers."

"He's a good dog!" Oskar asserted. "A very good dog!"

"Oh yes, Rusty is a good dog—none better!" Finn was quick to agree. "It's just that sometimes you need a specialist on the case, so we were called in to consult." Oskar nodded, and Finn continued, "You see, it can be painstaking work to detect the trail of one specific human from another. It can take a lot of time. But with a two-year-old child, you've got the diaper factor."

"Uh huh." Oskar nodded in agreement.

"The diaper factor?" I repeated questioningly.

"That's right," Finn continued. "Instead of looking for one particular human, you just look for a poopy diaper with a human attached. We found the little guy in about twenty minutes."

"Voila," Oskar added. "Safe and sound."

"Nice work, guys," I said. "That's a good tip. I'm going to remember that."

"Our pleasure, ranger. Happy to help," Finn said.

After our shift at the information desk, I was

scheduled to hold my first Bark Ranger training class. I had invited all the dogs I'd met at the desk that morning and told them to bring their families. It looked like most of them had decided to attend.

"Welcome to the first ever Bark Ranger training class," I barked to the group. "Who can tell me what B stands for?"

A petite forepaw belonging to a cute mini dachshund shot up immediately. "Bag it!" she said excitedly from her seat in the middle of the front row. "And then dispose of it in the proper trash receptacle because it doesn't do any good to bag it if you just leave the bags lying around all over the place, right?"

"Right! Very good. You really did your homework."

"Thank you. Conservation is very important to me. I come to this park a lot, and I want to help keep it clean and beautiful for my puppies to enjoy some day."

There were several yips of approval from the others in attendance. It was very encouraging. The whole class breezed through the rest of the training, and Ranger Mike and I presented the graduates with certificates that I signed with my paw print. I could see this program would really make a difference.

After the class, Ranger Mike and I grabbed a quick lunch and then headed out on Park Loop Road toward Ocean Drive. The parking lot at Sand Beach was packed, but that wasn't our responsibility. No dogs were allowed on the beach after June 15, and apparently that included junior rangers.

Our assignment was Thunder Hole, a half mile up Ocean Drive, and another of the most popular places in the park. Thunder Hole is a narrow inlet in the rock face that makes a sound like thunder when a wave hits it just right. Before you ask—no, I was not named after Thunder Hole. Apparently, I had larger than average paws as a puppy, and I have been told my name comes from the sound of my paws as I ran all around the house, but I guess it's more or less the same principle.

Thunder Hole sits smack in the middle of the Ocean Path, which is just about the most beautiful stretch of coastline you could ever want to see. That's why we have to patrol this area so heavily. Between drivers looking at the scenery and pedestrians looking at the scenery, someone has to be around to make sure they also look at each other. Our job today: Make sure no one gets run over.

"Excuse me, ranger. Is there a lightning hole somewhere too?" a woman asked Ranger Mike as we walked along the path. I couldn't wait to hear how Ranger Mike fielded that question, but unfortunately, I was called away on duty. Tempers can get short when so many dogs are trying to walk along the same path. You see, there are procedures to be observed in the canine world. You can't just breeze past all the tinkles and scratches that other dogs have left; it's rude. Traffic can get snarled, but that's not all that was getting snarled this afternoon.

"Hey, you already sniffed there," a burly bulldog said to a fragile-looking, middle-aged sheltie. "I'm trying to sniff there now, and I've only got a second. My mom is already tugging on my leash!"

"Oh, were you trying to sniff here?" she responded. "I'm sorry. I guess I lost my place. There's just so much to sniff, you know." She smiled politely.

Behind them, a Doberman yelped, "Come on, lady, sniff already."

"Yeah, lady, sniff it. Sniff it, and move on. Geesh!" a tiny Yorkie muttered under his breath.

"Take it easy, guys," I said to the line. "I'll

take care of this. Good afternoon, ma'am. May I be of assistance?"

"Why, thank you." The sheltie smiled sweetly at me. "What a nice young pup you are."

"Perhaps you'd like to sniff over here," I suggested, gently nudging her ahead a few yards, her people following along while still holding the leash. The bottleneck alleviated for now, the bulldog and the others grabbed a quick sniff and pulled their people forward at a hurried pace via relentless tension on their leashes. I shook my head—that's no way to tour the park. You've got to relax and take your time.

We spent the rest of our shift at Thunder Hole, managing traffic and pedestrians and, in general, keeping everything moving. Personally, I like this kind of work. I enjoy helping other dogs, and I like seeing them have a good time in the park. I couldn't help but notice, though, that every time I saw a golden retriever, it grabbed my attention. I knew this was one of Ciara's favorite places to bring her mom for a walk, and I guess I was hoping to see her and find out her plans for the holiday the next day.

Meanwhile, I saw a big, hairy Newfoundland coming toward me on the path. He looked pretty hot and tired, so I said, "You better rest a minute, buddy. You don't look so good."

"I'm h–h–h–hot," he panted, "and thirsty." I looked at his humans. They seemed oblivious to his distress, and I couldn't see that they were carrying any water at all. I barked for Ranger Mike to bring my water bottle.

"I've got some extra water," a spaniel passing the other way on the trail offered. She sat down and looked up at her human.

"Do you need a drink, Sparrow?" her human said, pulling a collapsible water bowl from her pack and filling it with water. "Your friend can have some too," she said, giving the Newfie a pat and then refilling the bowl for him twice.

"I'm good now, Ranger. Thanks," he said.

"No problem," I told him. I picked up the empty bowl and handed it to the spaniel. "Thanks, Sparrow. You can get a refill at Sand Beach. No dogs on the beach, but there's water by the restrooms." Then I caught a glimpse of something dark and fluffy darting across the road. "Gotta go," I said. "Enjoy your day!"

The fluffy black runaway turned out to be a sheep dog puppy that was almost my size but still just a baby. He had slipped out of his collar and was now weaving in and around the cars, trying to maneuver into the parking lot. His frantic humans chased after him calling, "Wait, Ishmael, wait!"

I cornered him in the parking lot. "What do you think you're doing, son?" I asked.

"We're playing Wait, Ishmael. I love this game!" he said. "It's almost as much fun as Stop It, Ishmael. That one is my favorite. I'm so lucky! My humans know a lot of games."

"Good for you, pup," I said, rolling my eyes a little, "but I think they're done playing for now." I led him back to his folks, who adjusted his collar a little tighter.

"He's just got so much hair," they said apologetically. "We didn't want to make it too tight."

They moved along, and I trotted back up the trail to join Ranger Mike. The sun was getting low in the sky, shining directly into my eyes and making it difficult to see, but was that—Yes! It was Ciara! She was in the back seat of her mom's car, and both of them were leaning out the window talking to Ranger Mike.

"Hi, Ciara!" I shouted enthusiastically, totally forgetting to be cool. I ran back up the trail and skidded to a stop just as the car began to move.

"Don't want to hold up traffic," her mom was

saying.

"See ya," Ciara yipped casually.

"Uh," I squeaked, and I stood there panting while the car drove away.

Ranger Mike looked at me and shook his head. "You know your ears are flipped over backwards, right?

CHAPTER 8

The village of Bar Harbor, Maine, was the best place in the whole country to celebrate Independence Day. The day began with blueberry pancakes served picnic style. This breakfast feast was very popular, and a line was already beginning to form when Ranger Mike and I arrived to help with the cooking. Most people don't know this, but Ranger Mike is a master pancake flipper. This morning he had a skillet in each hand, and he was flipping pancakes right and left, along with several other cooks. Volunteers hopped from grill to grill gathering up stacks of cooked pancakes and transporting them to the serving table. My job was to police the area for litter. Basically, that meant chasing down any paper cups or napkins that fell to the ground before they blew away. But bacon and sausage were also sizzling on the grills, and every so often a strip of bacon or a sausage link accidently hit the ground. Well, that was just edible litter, right? So, poised to spring, I scanned the air space under the grills for litter of any variety.

A sausage link had just hit the ground under grill two. I was on it in an instant, and I scarfed it down. Soon after, half a slice of crispy bacon fell from grill three. I was primed to spring, but my peripheral vision picked up another dog. Simultaneously, we pounced for the bacon, but when I saw who my competition was, I pull up in mid-air, stopping short of the prize.

"Help yourself to that bacon, Ciara."

She crunched it down. "Thank you." She smiled. "You know, I saw you save that puppy from getting lost yesterday on the Ocean Path. That was very sweet."

"Oh," I said, ducking my head, suddenly unable to look her in the eye. "Well, thanks…just doing my job."

"Are you helping with the fireworks tonight, Thunder? We could hang out after, or maybe I could join you on the clean-up or something."

"Sure, that'd be cool," I said, and she trotted off to join her family. Suddenly, the day's activities took on new meaning for me. I felt excited as I bounded over to help Ranger Mike finish the breakfast clean-up in time for the Fourth of July parade.

The parade was a central part of the celebration, and lots of park rangers and friends of Acadia participated. This year Ranger Mike and

I had a plum assignment. We would be riding in a horse-drawn carriage from Wildwood Stables. Draft horses lived at Wildwood in the summer and worked pulling wagon loads of visitors along the carriage roads in the park. Two of them were already hitched up to the carriage. I recognized Gus, one of the most experienced horses in the stable; I had worked with him before. I didn't know the other horse; he must have been new. I walked over to say hello. "Morning, guys," I called out.

Gus looked up from where he stood patiently waiting for the parade to start. "Morning, Thunder. Nice day for the parade," he whinnied as I approached. By contrast, the new guy stepped nervously in place as if he were preparing for a tap dance recital instead of a parade. "This is Fleet Feet Pete. He's a temp helping out for the holiday week."

"Fleet Feet Pete?"

"At your service," Pete said, snapping to attention.

"Pete's my cousin. He's a retired race horse. Made quite a name for himself in draft horse speed and strength events," Gus explained.

"Draft horses races? I've never heard of that," I said.

"It's kind of a specialty I suppose. Not a lot of coverage on ESPN or anything like that," Pete acknowledged.

"But if you're a draft horse, it's a really big deal," Gus was quick to add. "Pete here has been in the left front harness on the championship team three years running. The left front, Thunder! That's the lead horse on the team."

"Wow, that's impressive!"

"Thanks, guys. I appreciate the attention, but I'm retired now. I'm looking forward to taking it a little slower, stopping to smell the roses, you know."

"Sure. That sounds great, Pete," I said as I nodded.

The summit stewards would be riding with us, and I heard Charlie calling me from behind the carriage. "Thunder! Come on. It's time to line up for the parade." I trotted over. "Sit here by me," Charlie offered, patting the seat next to her. I hopped up, and Gus and Fleet Feet Pete pulled the carriage into the parade line right behind the bagpipe brigade and the giant lobster.

Up ahead, someone blew a loud whistle, and the color guard began to move forward, followed by one of the bright red Bar Harbor fire trucks loaded down with candy for the crowd of cheering spectators that lined the streets.

"Here we go!" Ranger Mike called from the driver's bench as he took the reins and signaled Gus and Fleet Feet to move forward. It was exhilarating! My tail was wagging so hard and fast that I couldn't keep my butt from wagging from side to side with it. I let out a couple of gleeful barks and smothered Charlie with kisses. Then I put my paws up on the side of the wagon to get a better view. Scanning the crowd, I recognized some of the kids I had met at the visitor center the day before scurrying along the sidewalk scooping up candy. I saw Finn and Oskar watching the parade with their family. They barked at me, and I barked back, caught up in the excitement of the moment.

We were approaching the first turn near the end of Main Street when Ranger Mike's cell phone began to ring. Later we would discuss that under the circumstances, "The Call to the Post" was not the best choice for a ringtone. However, it was equally unfortunate that an unauthorized firecracker went off with a loud bang just as our carriage rolled past. At the sound, Fleet Feet Pete pricked his ears, and his extensive training as an elite athlete took over. He lunged forward at full speed, and we were off to the races.

"Hey, where you going, dude?" Gus panted. "I can't keep up this pace!"

"I heard the starting pistol! This parade must be a race!" Pete gasped, whipping over to pass the bagpipers. "Come on, Gus. It's time to make our move!"

Spectators and passengers screamed as the carriage careened along Main Street. The giant lobster shouted, "Look out!" and the last row of the bagpipe brigade leapt out of our way, their kilts flapping up in the breeze as we blew past. One wheel of the carriage skidded into the curb. The resulting bump sent everyone on the left side of the carriage bouncing onto the floor.

"Ow," I yipped, my head spinning as I struggled to my feet. Too much to take in all at once, I caught flashes of the chaotic scene as if I were watching someone else's raw video on You Tube, rather than rolling around on the floor of the wagon myself. On the sidewalk, spectators surged back, giving the out-of-control carriage plenty of room. In the driver's seat, Ranger Mike struggled to stop the runaway horses. One of the stewards tried to help him control the team, but the wagon lurched to the side, sending him to the floor with the rest of us.

"Pete! You missed the turn!" Gus whinnied

frantically, the carriage now barreling downhill.

I was knocked off my paws again, and Charlie's face appeared in front of me. "Thunder, are you okay?" Behind her, the big moose on top of Geddy's was silhouetted against the clear blue sky. All at once, my head cleared, and I knew exactly where we were—heading straight for the waterfront!

I sprung to my paws. "Gus! Pull to the right, Gus!" I barked. Gus planted his hooves and leaned right. Fleet Feet Pete pivoted around him, effectively changing our direction. Great! Now we were not heading for the ocean—we were heading straight for the Bar Harbor Inn.

The slingshot effect from whipping around the corner sent everyone in the wagon sliding. The tailgate fell open, and Ranger Mike hollered, "Grab something and hang on!" Time switched to slow motion as I saw Charlie tumble toward the open tailgate. One of the stewards reached out to grab her hand as she rolled past, but the force of momentum quickly pulled it from his grasp. Frantically, Charlie grappled for a handhold.

"Charlie!" I barked. Lunging for her, I snapped my teeth shut on the back of her shorts just before she went summersaulting out of the carriage, digging my paws into the wooden floor as hard as I could. For a millisecond, we hung suspended in perfect balance, falling neither in nor out. Then I put everything I had into one last tug, shifting just enough molecules of air to redirect the energy my way, and we both fell back inside.

"Whew, that was close! Thanks, Thunder," Charlie said, scooting farther from the open tailgate. "Now, how are we going to stop this runaway?"

But even as the words left her mouth, the carriage came to a jolting stop. After making the loop around Agamont Park, we ended up right back on Main Street, at the corner of Main and Cottage. This prime parade viewing corner was packed with spectators, who all burst into loud cheers and applause.

"I guess everyone thinks that was part of the show," Charlie assessed.

"Did we win?" Fleet Feet Pete snorted.

"No, we didn't win. You can't win a parade— it's not a race! What got into you?" Gus demanded.

"But I heard the starting gun," Pete insisted.

The crowd parted, still cheering, to make way for us to return to the parade. Gus and Pete pulled the carriage back into line as the noise from the Shriners' go-carts drowned out their debate.

83

After the parade, the lobster races begin. Now, you might think I'd never want to hear the word race again after the parade, but I had a hot tip on a speedy lobster named Cariboo Snoots. I rushed over to the tanks to place my bet on the first race.

The master of ceremonies selected six kids from the audience to drop the contestants into the transparent race tank.

"Ready! Set! Go! And they're off!" he called. "Sticky Claws is out to an early lead with Butter Britches churning along on his tail. Mr. Pincher and Lobster Bob are poised to challenge, Snap Happy trails behind, and Cariboo Snoots is still at the starting line! Folks, I think he fell asleep. Meanwhile, Mr. Pincher is moving up to pass Butter Britches and challenge Sticky Claws for the lead. It's close folks, these two lobsters would be neck and neck if they had necks- But wait a minute! Back at the starting line, Cariboo Snoots is beginning to move. Wow, somebody really lit a fire under him. Snoots has crossed the midpoint, and it looks like Sticky Claws is all done as Snoots skims past and moves up to challenge Mr. Pincher, who has bogged down inches from the finish."

"Come on, Cariboo!" I barked excitedly. "You can do it!"

"This is going to be an exciting finish, folks. Cariboo Snoots is positioned to sneak right past Mr. Pincher. Oh! But wait, folks! I see some tail movement!" Inside the tank, Cariboo Snoots flipped his tail, a move that thrust him not forward but backward halfway across the tank.

"No!" I barked.

"Cariboo Snoots is out. He sent himself right back to the starting line, folks. Mr. Pincher wins the race!"

Next year, I'm betting on Mr. Pincher, I thought, making my way back to the picnic area with Ranger Mike.

We passed a mountain of corn on the cob waiting to be boiled and another mound of watermelons ready to be sliced. An ice chest was keeping fifty pounds of butter chilled, while enough hamburgers and hot dogs to feed the entire town sizzled on the grill.

Ranger Mike said, "Are you thinking what I'm thinking?"

"You bet I am," I barked. We followed the sublime aroma and got in line for the shore dinner behind a perky miniature dachshund, whom I recognized from my Bark Ranger class the previous day.

The dachshund lifted her nose to sniff the air. "I'm going to have two hamburgers and a hot dog," she mused out loud. "No! I'm going to have two hot dogs and a hamburger." She was very cute. Dapples of tan fur around her eyes and muzzle gave her an expressive face, while the tan fur on her paws made it look like she was wearing shoes. She turned her head to sniff again and noticed I was behind her in line. "Ranger Thunder! Hi! I was at your Bark Ranger seminar yesterday. Remember me? I'm Ponzie."

"Of course, Ponzie. It's nice to see you again." I smiled. "Tell me, can you really eat two burgers and a hot dog? All by yourself?"

"Oh, you heard that." She laughed. "I'm okay, really I am. I don't usually talk to myself out loud, but that food smells so good I can't make up my mind!"

"It does smell good," I agreed, hoping no drool was dripping out of my mouth.

"Besides, I wouldn't be eating it all by myself." She giggled at the confused look on my face and explained, "I'm expecting puppies at the end of the summer."

"Oh! Congratulations, Ponzie! How nice for you and your family."

"Yes, it really is, Thunder. It's doubly nice because my mom is expecting too! Oh, but not puppies of course. She's expecting a baby. We'll raise them together. It's going to be such fun!"

"Double congratulations. That does sound like fun," I told her warmly as her mom and dad picked up their food order and called her over to a table for lunch.

Ranger Mike and I were scheduled for patrol duty after lunch, so we each wolfed down a burger and hurried to our patrol truck. Lots of visitors mean lots of cars, so we were not surprised when our radio buzzed almost immediately and a voice chirped, "Ranger Mike. Come in, Ranger Mike."

"Ranger Mike here."

"The parking lot on top of Cadillac Mountain is completely full, and traffic is backing up. Nobody comes to the park to sit in a line of traffic. We've got to do something right away!"

"We're on it," Ranger Mike responded, pointing the truck in the direction of the Cadillac Mountain entrance. When we arrived, a long line of cars with idling motors and cranky honking drivers stretched all the way from Route 3 up the winding mountain road to the top. We parked our truck off the road and walked over to the first car that was still outside the entrance.

"Good afternoon, sir," Ranger Mike said to the driver. "The road is temporarily closed due to traffic."

"But we want to drive up the mountain to see the view," the driver explained.

"Yes, sir, we'll reopen the road as soon as we get things moving again, but it might take a while. No point waiting here in traffic when there are plenty of other great places to explore."

The driver nodded, sensibly acknowledging that waiting in traffic was no way to spend a holiday weekend, and moved on down the highway. Ranger Mike gave the same explanation to the next few cars until the entrance area was clear enough to close the gate and post a sign saying, "Road Temporarily Closed."

Then Ranger Mike turned his attention to the line of cars already waiting on the mountain road. One of the drivers cut off his engine and got out. We recognized him as the man who had asked us about roller coasters at the visitor center the day before.

"Hey, ranger! What's the holdup?"

"Sorry, sir, the parking lot is full on top of the mountain. Traffic will start to move again as soon as some of the cars on top come back down. I see a few already," Ranger Mike said, pointing to some cars in the distance.

"Honk!" a horn blasted from another car.

"Excuse me," Ranger Mike said, walking over to the honking car. "We're clearing traffic as quickly as possible," he explained. "That horn honking really isn't going to help any–"

"Beep!"

"Onnnk!"

"Beep!"

Pretty soon there was a whole symphony of horns honking music like I had previously only heard performed by geese. Ranger Mike and I were running back and forth, trying to keep everyone calm as cars trickled down the mountain, making room for the line to move up a few feet at a time. We kept this up for half an hour or so until finally the line of traffic had moved up to the first of the hairpin turns on the mountain road. Ranger Mike was directing a large RV that couldn't quite make the sharp turn without scraping cars in the other lane. Over on the side of the road, a couple of chipmunks were having a good time watching the show.

"Bigger RVs," one of them said, pointing and

laughing. "That's what you need, Ranger."

"Yeah," the other chipmunk chimed in, "maybe even some of those double-decker buses."

"You two aren't helping the situation here, you know," I paused to tell them.

"Help!" the first chipmunk chortled. "Why should we help? We're thinking about selling tickets!"

"Yeah, this is the best show in town," his partner agreed.

"You can't sell tickets. You may recall I reminded you just two weeks ago that concessions require a special use permit. No permits can be issued unless–"

"Excuse me, ranger." A curly-haired terrier had walked up behind me.

I looked over my shoulder at him. "We're clearing the road as quickly as possible," I said. "Please, wait in your car. It shouldn't be long."

"Yes, I was waiting in my car, but I had to get out to poop, and–"

"Fine," I said. "Just bag it and tag it."

"Yes, I bagged it, but I thought you might want to know–"

"Yes, yes, good boy, thanks for telling me," I

said, barely paying any attention to him at all.

"No, I didn't think you'd want to know about the poop," he persisted. "I thought you'd want to know about the bus."

"Uh-huh," I responded without looking in his direction, my attention still divided between the chipmunks and the cars backing up to allow more room in the switchback. "This traffic jam is dangerous, especially for small rodents. Now, I need you chipmunks to back up a few more feet from the road. I don't want anyone getting hurt."

"I thought you'd want to know about the bus because of the fire," the terrier insisted.

My ears pricked straight up. Now he had my attention. "Fire!" I yelped. "What fire?"

The terrier pointed with his paw to a bus a few cars behind the wedged camper. "That bus is on fire," he said.

CHAPTER 9

Adrenaline saturated my blood, tensing every muscle in my body. I launched myself toward the bus, barking the alarm at full volume. Ranger Mike had just managed to unsnarl the cars enough to get the RV some room to maneuver, and the line of backed-up vehicles began moving down the mountain again.

"Woof–woof–woof–woof–woof!" I barked sharply as I ran. The bus moved forward. I could see flames peeking out from underneath one of the front wheels as it rolled right past me without stopping. I did a one-eighty and charged after it. "Woof–woof–woof–woof–woof!"

I bounded past Ranger Mike, almost knocking him off his feet.

"Hey! Thunder! Get back here!" he called after me, but then he saw the flames and fell in behind me, chasing after the bus. "Stop!" he cried. "Stop the bus!"

The bus driver finally pulled over. "What's up, ranger? Why'd you stop us?" he asked.

Ignoring his question, Ranger Mike jumped aboard the bus. "Everyone off the bus!" he ordered.

"But, ranger, the tour isn't over," a lady in the front seat said with exasperation. "We have three more stops."

"Please, ma'am, for your own safety, get off the bus immediately!" Ranger Mike grabbed the fire extinguisher that was mounted by the door of the bus and ran around to the driver's side wheel, using the extinguisher to put out the flames.

"The brakes must have overheated," the driver hypothesized, examining a charred area around the wheel well. "What now, ranger? How do I get this bus down the mountain with no brakes?"

"Uh, that's a good question." With horns honking and a couple of drivers hollering suggestions in the background, Ranger Mike keyed the radio on his shoulder. "Dispatch, I need backup on Cadillac. Can you send Ranger Bob?"

"Ranger Bob is working a rescue on the Beehive. A lady is stuck at the ladder. She's afraid to go across, but she can't go back because people are backed up the trail from waiting for her to move," the dispatcher explained.

"Yikes! That doesn't sound good. How about Ranger Diana? Can you send Ranger Diana?"

"Ranger Diana found a couple of kids who got lost on the way to the restrooms. She helped them find their campsite, but apparently the parents went looking for them, so now Ranger Diana is looking for the parents."

"Jeepers!" Ranger Mike exclaimed.

"Yeah, welcome to the Fourth of July at Acadia, Ranger Mike," the dispatcher said. "I'll send someone as soon as I can."

"Roger," Ranger Mike acknowledged. He pulled out his cell and tapped in a number. "Send the biggest tow truck you have," he said into the phone, "big enough to haul a tour bus down Cadillac Mountain." Then he looked down at me. "Thunder, we've got to figure out a way to clean up this mess on our own."

"Right!" I barked. "I'm on it!"

While Ranger Mike rounded up the bus passengers, I ran back up the line of cars, stopping to smile and wag my tail at each one to let the occupants know we were working on the problem. When people reached out to pet me, I obliged them by putting my paws up on the car door, being careful not to scratch the paint of course. Stress relief—that's what you call that in psychology, and it works both ways, lowering people stress and dog stress.

I approached a bright red Smart car; I was surprised when twin tri-colored Bermers poked their heads out from the tiny back seat.

"Hey, ranger!" they said in unison.

"Wow, you guys okay in there?" I asked.

"Sure, we're fine," one said.

"Yeah, we'd just like to go," the other supplied.

"My partner and I are working on it," I assured them. "It shouldn't be much longer." Their humans reached out to pet me.

"Would you like a treat, Ranger Dog?" the driver asked, pulling out a huge dog biscuit shaped like a bone.

"Thanks!" I barked, accepting the cookie, but for once I didn't crunch right into it. In the window of the car ahead, I could see the terrier who had alerted me to the bus fire. I walked up to his window and offered him the big dog biscuit.

"Thanks for the heads-up, terrier. You were a real hero today."

"Aw, it was nothing, ranger," he responded humbly, but I could tell he was pleased with himself as he crunched into the cookie with a big smile.

"Enjoy the rest of your visit to Acadia," I said.

The tow truck arrived in record time and hauled the bus away, and the tour company sent two vans from Island Taxi to pick up the passengers to finish their tour. With the bus out of the way, the cars on top of Cadillac were able to come down, and the cars still waiting at the bottom could now make their way up to the top. When Ranger Mike and I reopened the road a few minutes later, everything was back to normal.

Ranger Mike turned to me. "I guess we handled that!" he said.

"Yeah, we did, partner!" I yelped. With a high five, and a paw bump, we were back on patrol. We drove over to Eagle Lake, a popular place for kayaking and cycling, and posted ourselves at the carriage road intersection. Within a few minutes, more than a dozen bicycles had passed. People were having a good time. They waved as they passed, and a couple even stopped to give me a pat on the head.

A man riding a bicycle with a bright green box-like contraption strapped onto the back pulled over to ask Ranger Mike a question. I had never seen anything like this box. It was open on the top and three sides, but the open part was covered in black mesh. It looked like a screened-in porch for a hobbit house. I crept up to get a better look, and since I mostly look with my nose, I was sniffing the mesh enclosure when a big black paw whacked me on the muzzle.

"Ow," I said a bit indignantly, rubbing my nose.

"Who do you think you're sniffing, nosey?" a disembodied feline voice challenged from somewhere behind the mesh.

"Pardon me, madam. I didn't know you were in there."

"Well, now you do, so why don't you back that vacuum cleaner snout of yours away a few feet so I can breathe? What good does it do me to be out in the fresh air with my chauffer when you're sucking up all the oxygen like a kid with a straw chasing the last drop of chocolate milk around the bottom of the carton?"

"Sorry," I said, backing away to join Ranger Mike.

"Is my cat, Miss Fortune, eligible to be a Bark Ranger?" the cat's human, or family, or chauffer, or whatever he was, was asking Ranger Mike.

"Well, now, that's a good question. We never thought about cats becoming Bark Rangers, but I don't see why not," Ranger Mike said thoughtfully. *Nooooo!* I waved my paws in the air while shaking my head from side to side—*Not that cat!*—but my partner was oblivious. "We have training scheduled for 1 p.m. tomorrow at the nature center at Sieur de Monts." I paw-slapped my forehead. *Great. Looks like I'm training a cat.* The cat's human thanked Ranger Mike and turned my direction. I plastered a smile on my face and offered a halfhearted tail wag.

"Nice doggy," he said uncomfortably, his lip curling into a sneer. Then he patted me on the head as if I had poison ivy growing out of my ears. Before mounting his bicycle, he leaned down and spoke to the mesh box in baby talk. "Is Daddy's little princess having a good time in the park? Who's Daddy's precious kitty?"

"Meow," the cat said sweetly. "Meow." Then, as the man peddled away, she called back to me, "See you tomorrow, nosey."

"Isn't that nice?" Ranger Mike said. "I'm glad the Bark Ranger program is attracting some interest from feline visitors."

I stared at him with my mouth open.

"Maybe we should have a special designation for cats since cats don't really bark," he mused.

"How about calling them Hairball Rangers," I yipped. "They hack up plenty of those."

Ranger Mike checked his watch. "Better get back to town. It'll be time for the fireworks soon, and don't forget, we're on clean-up duty." How could I forget? I had been looking forward to seeing Ciara after the fireworks all day.

* * *

Downtown was abuzz with activity and was literally swarming with people and dogs making their way toward the pier for the concert and fireworks. I love crowds. I'm a people dog, or a dog person, or...well, I'm not sure how to say it, but what I mean is, I find weaving through crowds of happy people and smiling dogs fun and exhilarating.

We took up our post across from the town pier, next to the Bar Harbor Inn. The band was already on stage, and the lawn was packed with families picnicking, lounging on blankets, or sitting in lawn chairs, enjoying the show. The Shore Path also provided a good view and was lined with spectators, while still more people watched from their balconies at the Bar Harbor Inn. The sky was clear and growing darker by the minute. It was a perfect night for a spectacular fireworks display.

At the end of the concert, the crowd applauded enthusiastically but grew quiet again soon after the band left the stage. Everyone turned their attention to the sky. With each passing moment, the atmosphere grew more electric with anticipation of the grand finale. Thunk. The expectant silence was broken by the sound of muffled artillery. Thunk, thunk was followed by woosh, woosh, and everyone held their breath. Then, suddenly, vivid starbursts and sparkling chrysanthemums exploded across the sky. They continued one after the other, followed by trails of sparks sizzling and crackling back down to the ground. The fireworks went on for some time, each element bigger and more brilliant than the last. The enthralled spectators oohed and ahhed until the display ended in spectacular fashion with dozens of wooshes and thunks filling the sky with an enormous bouquet of magnificent, sparkling flowers. It was an impressive display, and the crowd whooped and cheered their appreciation.

As the smoke dispersed and drifted away, people gathered their belongings to do likewise. I heard snippets of conversations, like "Amazing" and "Best display ever," but suddenly I heard one panicked voice raised above the rest.

"Macy! Macy, where are you?" a man shouted from nearby. "Help! I can't find my little girl!"

Ranger Mike and I rushed over to help.

Pulling out his notebook, Ranger Mike began firing questions at the frantic father. "What's her full name? How old is she? When was the last time you saw her?"

A moment later, two Bar Harbor police officers joined the scene with a Hancock County deputy sheriff. Now they were all firing question and making notes. *Somebody should start looking for the kid,* I thought. So I began sniffing around, working on sorting out the scent of the parents, the cops, and the other people in the vicinity as I worked my way down to the scent of the little girl. That's when I remembered the tip I had gotten from Finn and Oskar back at the visitor center the day before. *The diaper factor! Of course!*

I pulled my nose up off the ground, pointed it into the air, and sniffed. *Whoa!* I got something right away. I let out a quick yelp to alert the others, and I took off running. My nose led me straight to the big flower beds on the back side of the Bar Harbor Inn, and there she was, both hands full of yellow flowers. "Doggie!" she exclaimed in greeting, and I gave her a little kiss. The diaper factor—it never fails!

I was happy, of course, that we had found Macy quickly—my duty as a junior park ranger comes before anything else—but I was disappointed

I hadn't had time to look for Ciara after the fireworks. Most of the crowd had already cleared out, returning to their hotels or campsites. Ranger Mike and the cops were doing paperwork about the missing child incident, leaving me to handle the clean-up by myself. Normally, I wouldn't mind because I actually like clean-up duty. You never know what you're going to find. Half-eaten pudding cups, peanut butter and jelly sandwiches...once I had found a whole package of cheesy crackers. But I had been looking forward to seeing Ciara all day, and it was disappointing to have missed the opportunity. Even though my heart wasn't in it, I began combing the area for leftover tidbits.

"Hi, Thunder. Looks like you could use some help."

"Ciara! You waited for me!"

"Sure. I figured it was the only way I'd get to see you. You're a very busy dog, Thunder. I never realized what it takes to be a junior park ranger, but I'm starting to now."

I could feel myself standing a little taller as she spoke...and probably turning a little redder too. "I think I saw half a bucket of popcorn over by the cannons. Want to help me clean it up?"

"Sure," she said with a smile.

We took care of the popcorn and then finished off a couple of discarded ice cream cones that had missed the trash can. "That's about it, I guess." I was a little reluctant to end the evening, but I had another full day tomorrow.

"Come on. I'll walk you home," Ciara said. We strolled back down Main Street, which was almost empty now, then cut through the village green and turned toward our neighborhood on the outskirts of town. We were home in no time.

"Thanks for waiting, Ciara."

"My pleasure, Thunder. See you around."

"Yeah, sure, see you around." I entered through the junior ranger door and walked straight to my bed. Spot was in it. *She's probably slept eighteen hours today, and I've been on duty since 6 a.m.* I was too tired to spar with her tonight, so I looked around for another place to sleep.

"Come on, Thunder. You can bunk with me tonight," Ranger Mike offered. I hopped onto the bed, and we were both asleep as soon as our heads hit the pillows.

CHAPTER 10

Miss Fortune, the long-haired black Persian I'd met in her custom bicycle seat the day before, sat perched on a tree stump behind the Sieur de Monts Nature Center, her paw in the air with yet another interruption.

"I can't keep up with the presentation material," she whined. "Maybe you could get something to *point* with so I can follow along. You know, like a *pointer*."

"For the last time," I said, speaking slowly and deliberately, "I don't *need* a pointer. I *am* a pointer. Seriously, it's what I do. Now, please, try to pay attention. We've been at this for almost half an hour, and we're still on B for bag it."

"But, ranger, who bags it? I mean, I'm *willing* to bag it, you understand, but no thumbs, you see. I'm *physiologically* unable to bag it."

This morning, Ranger Mike had suggested that Spot come along and be certified as a Bark Ranger cat too. "Our visiting cat will be more comfortable with another cat in the class," he'd said, and I had to admit he was right. I was coming unglued, of course, but so far, both cats seemed pretty comfortable.

Spot raised her paw. "I'm allergic to plastic bags," she protested.

"If you can't bag it, get your human to bag it. Now, please, can we move on to the next point?"

"You're the pointer," Miss Fortune purred.

I ignored that crack and moved on. "Okay, next we have A. That stands for 'always wear a leash.' Now, this is for your protection. It's easy to get into trouble out there." Both cats raised their paws immediately.

"A leash doesn't really go with this collar."

"Just a leash, right? Not a collar, because collars chafe my neck."

"Does someone have to hold the other end of the leash, or is that optional?"

"You said something about trouble.... I don't like trouble unless I'm causing it."

"Well, if you don't like trouble, then you're going to want to wear a leash—a leash with a collar and with someone holding the other end. Now, any more questions?"

"Excuse me, ranger!"

"Yes, Spot?"

"I'm allergic to plastic collars."

"Then get a leather collar. Can we move on now?"

"You're leading the class," she said innocently.

"I'm not sure that's really true, but let's move on anyway. The next letter is R. That stands for 'respect wildlife.' Now, ladies, you are aware that wildlife includes birds and lizards, right?" I peered over at them. Both cats were now sitting up very straight with angelic looks on their faces. I could swear I saw halos hovering over their heads as they nodded politely.

"Moving on... Lastly, we have K. That stands for 'know where you can go.' No leashes are allowed on the ladder trails." Both cats' paws shot up.

"Spot?"

"I don't need a leash to get up a ladder trail."

"That's not the point—"

"I don't need a leash to get up any ladder."

"Neither do I," Miss Fortune interjected. "I can climb anything."

"I can climb anything too—and fast," Spot insisted.

"Um, excuse me, ladies, please—" I tried to

cut in but both cats ignored me.

"You think you can climb faster than me?" Miss Fortune challenged incredulously.

"I don't know about you. I just know I climb faster than every other cat I've ever met," Spot countered.

"That's big talk, Missy. Care to prove it?" Miss Fortune shrilled, her voice raised an entire octave.

Uh oh! I didn't like where this was going. "Okay, okay, class is over. Thank you for supporting—"

"You see that big white pine? We'll see who climbs fast around here!" Spot hissed.

"Ranger Mike!" I barked. "I'm in over my head here! Ranger Mike! Anybody! Ranger needs backup!"

**

Later that afternoon, Ranger Mike and I were checking cairns on Cadillac. We had hiked almost to the top via the North Ridge Trail when a group of hikers on the way down stopped us to ask Ranger Mike a question. While he was chatting with them, I scanned the area for a ripe blueberry or two. I spotted one and daintily plucked it from the bush. It was perfect, so sweet and juicy. I spied another and another, and you know how it goes. Anyway, that's what I was doing when I heard a frantic rustling in the bushes on the other side of a wide expanse of granite. Something about that noise grabbed my attention. I directed my eyes and ears toward the bush, and my powerful nose began taking in and categorizing information like a computer: soil, rocks, lichens, pine sap, berries, BIRD! Without any conscious effort, my entire body stiffened as I pointed my nose and my paw precisely where my finely tuned instincts told me a bird was hiding under a blueberry bush. Slowly and silently I advanced on the bush, my movements so measured and precise as to be almost imperceptible.

Now, I know generally it's the feline who enjoys a reputation as a cold and calculating silent stalker. But as a bird dog, I have to tell you, our ability to advance in complete stealth mode, a millimeter at a time if that's what it takes, is second to none in the animal world. Of course, I can understand how that might be difficult to believe if you have ever received an enthusiastic greeting from a bird dog. We greet you wagging not only our tails but our entire bodies. We greet you as if you had been gone eight years rather than eight hours. We greet you as if we had last seen you on the deck of the Titanic, with little hope of ever seeing you again. But don't let that fool you. Cats have nothing on us when it comes to stalking in stealth mode. Patience and self-control are our bread and butter.

So I was advancing on the bush with extreme caution, but even so, I couldn't have been more surprised by what I found when I carefully nudged the leaves aside. It was a falcon, a peregrine falcon to be precise. I'd know one anywhere: slate gray wings, a mottled gray and white chest, and a dark toupee with long sideburns. Apex predators and the fastest animals on Earth, they are also the Elvis impersonators of the animal kingdom. These birds are usually seen soaring high in the sky or stooping toward Earth at two hundred miles per hour. This bird, however, fluttered helplessly on the ground.

"Falcon! I'm sorry to surprise you like this!" His fluttering became more frantic when he saw me. "Don't worry. I'm here to help. I'm a junior park ranger. My name is Thunder."

He had been struggling to straighten some disheveled feathers on his left wing. Now he stopped flapping and tucked his wings as best he could. Sitting up straight on his imposing raptor talons, he turned his dark, round eyes on me.

A falcon's eyes are precision instruments, affording them the visual acuity to see prey from a mile away. But this falcon seemed to be using his to stare right through me, attempting to visually assess my trustworthiness.

"Thun-dare?" he questioned suspiciously when he finally spoke, revealing a melodious French accent. "But surely you are a bird dog, monsieur." As a junior ranger, it's my job to know about protected animals. Falcons and other birds of prey have been protected since they were almost wiped out by a pesticide called DDT, which poisoned their food supply.

"Yes, I'm a bird dog, but I'm still a junior ranger, and I've sworn an oath to preserve and protect this park and everything in it. You can trust me," I assured him. "I would never break my oath."

The bird paused for another moment, and then he let out a big sigh. The irony of his predicament was obvious. Still, I was his best hope for assistance, and however unlikely, he really had no choice but to trust me.

CHAPTER 11

"You see, Thun-dare, peregrines, we are... how you say? Misunderstood. People say we dive so fast, we strike in mid-air, and we have terrifying, razor-sharp talons! This is, of course, true, but it is also true that our strike rate is very low. You see, if I stoop five targets, I will likely only bring one home."

"You're right. I didn't know that," I acknowledged.

"So, you see, Julia and I– Ah," he interrupted himself, "Julia she is my mate, and I am Perrot. So, as I was saying," he continued, "Julia and I, we like this area—how you call it?—Acadia, very much. We hatched two eggs and fledged both chicks here last year. So this year, when we were planning our migration, we said, why not go back to Acadia? It was a beautiful place, and we had a successful nest. So we fly back here and scratch a nest on the same cliff as last year. Everything is good. Julia, she lays, would you believe, three eggs! And we hatch all three eggs! We are so very happy. Such good fortune! We take turns tending the chicks, hunting the food, and guarding the nest. The chicks, they grow, they eat more food, and soon I start to think, this is a big responsibility. I worry that I cannot bring home enough food. I start to take more chances, hunting longer and in unfamiliar areas. And then yesterday, I was hunting from quite high up, just soaring along, floating on thermals over the Bowl—you know, the lake behind Champlain Mountain—when I spotted some targets banking off to the north. It was a large group. I tracked with my eyes for a few seconds, watching them fly across the gorge and angle up to gain altitude heading toward Cadillac. I plotted an intercept course and dove after them. Pulling my wings in tight, leaving just enough exposed feather to steer, I was closing in at about 220 miles per hour— maybe even a bit more. This speed, it is no problem for me, Thun-dare. I fly this fast easily. I had my eyes trained on the target, my trajectory was clear, and there was just wide-open space between me and my prize—or so I thought. Just as I was about to strike, something knocked me right out of the sky. You see, I had forgotten there is a road for cars on this mountain. I tell you, Thun-dare, look both ways before you fly across the road."

"I'll remember that." I nodded. "Perrot, how badly are you hurt?"

He sighed again. "I am done for, Thun-dare. Look at my wing." He held his left wing out as far as he could for me to see. Several of the long flight feathers near his left wing tip were bent or broken, poking out at odd angles. I knew from the flight lecture Cooper and I had gotten from the gull that day on Bar Island that Perrot could not fly with his feathers in that condition.

"I'm still a young falcon," he went on, "but that is not the real tragedy. The real tragedy is that without my help, our nest is almost sure to fail. The three chicks will die, and Julia will not know what happened. She may think I abandoned the nest—something I would never do—but how will she know?" He looked down and scratched at the thin layer of dirt covering the granite mountain that somehow was not only enough to sustain the blueberries but was their preferred habitat.

"Don't give up yet, Perrot. I'll get Ranger Mike. He'll take you to Acadia Raptor Rehab."

***

An hour later, we were headed toward the raptor rehab center with Perrot on the seat between us in a ventilated animal transport box. Our radio

113

chirped. "Go ahead," Ranger Mike responded.

"Ranger Bruce here. The male falcon from the nest on the Precipice hasn't been seen since yesterday morning. Dispatch said you were bringing in an injured falcon. Does the injured bird have a tag?"

"Affirmative, a green wildlife tag marked B17."

"That's him," Ranger Bruce responded, his concern apparent. "Please advise regarding his condition."

"Roger," Ranger Mike responded into the radio. Perrot looked up at me as Ranger Mike lifted the transport box out of the truck. I nodded reassuringly. It was good that the other rangers knew Perrot was the father of the chicks in the Precipice nest. At least now we were all on the same page.

Inside the center, a woman was sitting on a stool by the window, holding a furry brown bat. She was using tweezers to feed tiny mealworms to the bat from a bowl in her lap. "Hello," she said when we walked in. "It's bat snack time."

"We've got an emergency here, an injured peregrine," Ranger Mike announced. "We picked him up on the north side of Cadillac, near the road.

Judging by the location, it may have been a vehicle strike."

"Let's take a look," she said, returning the bat to its enclosure. She put the bowl of worms into a small refrigerator. "By the way, I'm River. I'm a certified wildlife rehabber for raptors and for some other animals. Right now I'm trying to give the bats around here a hand. There's a very serious problem with white nose fungus." She washed her hands then opened the carrier and carefully placed Perrot on the examination table. "His injuries appear to be confined to the left wing." She held Perrot's wing out to assess the extent of the damage. "This entire section of flight feathers near the wing tip is broken or bent beyond use. It's a serious injury. There's no way he can fly like this. I'm afraid he's grounded until these feathers molt and new ones grow in, several weeks at least, maybe months. He can stay here until he grows some new feathers." We followed as she carried Perrot outside. "What a handsome falcon you are," she said, placing him in a large enclosure. "I'll take good care of him," she assured us.

In the cage, Perrot sat perched on a branch, his head hanging low in a very un-falcon-like posture. I wanted to offer some comfort, but I had no idea what I could say that might help. When I thought about what Perrot had at stake, I could feel my own head drooping too. A few weeks off his wings would likely cost him his whole family. "Hmm, hmm, hmm," I whined softly.

"This falcon has an active nest with three chicks. It's almost sure to fail without him," Ranger Mike spoke up. "Every chick is so important to the falcon program. Is there anything you can do to help him get back in the air?"

"Well," she paused thoughtfully, "there is one thing we could try. But I'm telling you right now, it's a long shot." Perrot lifted his head and looked over at me, a glimmer of hope in his sharp eyes. "It's called imping, and it's an old technique that was developed when falconry and hunting with falcons was popular. The damaged part of each feather is cut off, and a replacement feather is glued right into the shaft. But the whole thing hinges on finding the right type of feathers in the right size. I don't have any feathers here, and the procedure won't work unless we can find a match for each damaged feather. I can't promise anything, but I will start looking for donor feathers immediately."

For the rest of the day, Ranger Mike and I were on pins and needles waiting for River to call. I stared at the radio in the patrol truck while Ranger Mike repeatedly checked his cell phone for messages. We were so antsy that when the phone finally rang, we about jumped out of our skin.

"A bird sanctuary in Lewiston has left wing falcon feathers that might be a match," River said. "I have a room full of hungry bats that have to be fed by hand, but I'll go pick up the feathers as soon as I'm finished."

I looked at Ranger Mike intently. "Hmm, hmm, hmm," I pleaded.

"Don't worry about it, River. You feed the bats, and Thunder and I will retrieve the feathers." I smiled and gave him a wag. He rolled down my window, and I turned my face into the breeze as we headed south on Route 1. I thought we should use the siren too, but I guess that might have been overkill.

It was a long drive, but we made good time and returned with the feathers sealed in a hard, plastic case that protected them from being damaged.

River opened the cage and carefully put Perrot up on the table. "Let's see what we've got to work with here." She picked up the sterile scissors and cut one of the bent feathers from Perrot's left wing, being careful to remove the damaged part, but leave the feather shaft. "If he had lost the whole feather, we wouldn't be able to do the splice. There's no way to embed a donor feather into the skin."

She opened the box, took out some of the feathers, and compared them to the damaged feather tip she had just removed. "It's a match!" she announced triumphantly. She selected from among the feathers in the box to find the right match for each of the damaged feathers. One by one, she carefully trimmed and glued the new feathers inside the shafts of the old feathers. When she was finished, you could barely tell the feathers had been replaced other than the new feathers made a slightly different pattern, appearing to be more speckled than the pattern of Perrot's original feathers.

"So far, so good." River smiled. "We'll let the glue dry a few hours, and then I'll transfer him to a flight enclosure overnight so he can try them out. If that goes well, we can release him in the morning."

***

The next morning, Perrot greeted me enthusiastically. "Thun-dare! Look at my wing! It is as good as new!"

"It looks perfect, Perrot. How does it feel?"

"It feels great! I'm still a little stiff from the accident, but the wing feels strong, I'm sure I can fly with it. I can't tell you what it means to me to get back to my nest and help Julia feed our chicks. I'll never forget your kindness, Thun-dare."

"I'm happy we were able to help, Perrot. Give my regards to your family."

"Okay, here we go," River said, unlocking the latch and pulling open the wide screened door that allowed access to open sky. "Come on, Falcon B17. Show us how it's done."

Perrot took a moment to stretch his wings and fluff out his feathers. Then he gave me a wink and leapt into the sky. Soaring out over town toward the bay, he gained altitude in a wide arc then banked sharply off to the south, toward his home and family on the precipice of Champlain Mountain.

CHAPTER 12

It had been a busy summer at Acadia, and now, with the last day of August approaching, the park was shifting into autumn mode. Ranger Mike and I had continued to train new Bark Rangers all summer. We discontinued the cat ranger program, however, right after we managed to get Spot and Miss Fortune down from the tall white pine behind the Sieur de Monts Nature Center.

Ranger Bruce continued to monitor the Precipice nest after Perrot returned, or Falcon B17 as the other rangers called him. All three of the chicks had survived and were now fully fledged adolescent falcons currently getting hunting lessons from their parents.

I loved autumn, or fall, like my mama always called it. Something about the crisp, cool air felt exhilarating and made me walk a little taller on my paws. But the end of summer meant saying goodbye to my friends, the summit stewards, including my good friend Charlie. We had forged a close relationship while learning about the park together and passing that information on to the many visitors we met along the way. I was going to miss her, but I knew it was time for her to return to college and to continue mapping out a bright future for herself. This night we were showing our appreciation to the stewards and other seasonal employees with a combination end-of-season celebration and going-away party.

"I'm going to miss you, Thunder!" Charlie gave me a big hug and the crust from her pizza. "I hope we can work together again next summer."

Me too, I thought, finishing my crust. I gave her a big kiss.

I was feeling happy later that night when Ranger Mike and I got into our truck to drive home. That feeling changed quickly to concern when we came upon the red tail lights of an SUV that had run off the road and down a steep embankment. I wish I could say it was an unusual sight, but there's something about the combination of unfamiliar roads and stunning scenery that leads to our fair share of accidents on Mount Desert Island. Ranger Mike pulled the truck off the road and called 911.

"Accident on Kebo Mountain Road," he said, jumping out of truck. "Send an ambulance." I followed him to the scene, where we slid down the steep bank to try to help the people inside the vehicle. Inside, I could see a man and a woman.

Neither was moving, but my nose told me they were both alive.

Up on the street, another car pulled over, and Ciara's mom got out. "I'll be right down to help!" she called. Grabbing her doctor's bag, she made her way down the embankment. I walked back up to wait by the car with Ciara.

"My mom is a doctor. She can help," Ciara said, reading the look of concern on my face. "It looks like a bad accident."

"Yes, the car is nose down in the brook. It almost flipped completely over!"

We could hear sirens now and could see the spinning red lights of the emergency vehicles speeding our way. The paramedics took the woman out of the car and carried her up to the waiting ambulance, which sped away as soon as the doors were slammed shut. Overhead, we could hear the whop-whop sound of a helicopter.

"They must be taking her to meet the helicopter at the athletic field," Ciara said. "My mom says the helicopter comes when you have to get to the hospital fast."

A second ambulance arrived on the scene, and this time the paramedics pulled a man from the car. They loaded him onto a gurney and carried it up the embankment.

"What happened? Where's, my wife?" He mumbled over and over, "my wife is she ok? Is Ponzie, okay? Did somebody get her out? What about my wife?" My ears pricked up. *Did he say Ponzie?* The man was groggy and his voice muffled by an oxygen mask. It was difficult to make out what he was saying, but I thought I heard him say Ponzie.

"Don't worry. They already took your wife to the hospital," the EMT said in a soothing voice. Then she shut the doors, and the ambulance sped away, siren wailing.

"Did he say Ponzie?" I asked Ciara, the alarm in my voice signaling my high state of alert.

"I'm not sure. What is it, Thunder? What's wrong?"

"Wait here. I need to check that car for another passenger!" The tow truck had arrived, and the driver was attaching chains and tow ropes to the back of the car, but the front doors were still open. I poked my head inside the car. "Ponzie! Ponzie! Are you in there?" I barked. Looking around the SUV, there was no sign of a dog inside, but I was still pretty sure it was her car; it smelled dachshundy. Then I saw an open bag of dog treats laying right out in plain sight on the passenger side floor. Strong evidence a dog, probably Ponzie, must have been there—but where had she gone? Was she hurt? She had left without the bag of treats. Only a dog in serious trouble, desperate even, would have left that bag behind.

"Out of the way, pooch. Time to haul this car out," the tow truck driver ordered, his hands on the door, ready to slam it shut. I yelped my assent and started to back myself out of his way, but at the last second, I reached back in and snagged the treat bag. Slam! The door whizzed past my face, blowing my ears back and narrowly missing the bag of treats clenched in my teeth.

When I got back to the car, Ciara said, "What was that all about?"

"Meet me in my backyard in half an hour. We need to organize a search party—a dachshund is missing!"

Half an hour later, Ciara stepped through the rhododendrons and into the back yard, where I was waiting with Cooper. "I had to get my mom settled down after that accident," she said. "I gave her a book. That will keep her busy for hours." A few minutes later, Reggie's dad opened the door, and Reggie trotted over.

"Thanks for coming, everybody," I began. "Ciara and I saw a bad accident on Kebo Mountain Road tonight. Two humans were taken to the hospital, but I have reason to believe there was also a dog in the car, a dachshund named Ponzie. If she was in the car, she's gone missing, and she could be hurt. The quicker we start searching, the better chance we have of finding her. Can you all help search tonight?" I asked, but they were already on their feet.

"Let's go," Reggie said. "We're wasting time!"

We galloped back to the scene of the accident. All the emergency vehicles and flashing lights were gone now, and the tow truck had hauled the wrecked Subaru away. Shattered glass sparkled from a patch of flattened greenery on the creek bank. Not much else was left at the scene but some broken plastic from the headlights, on the ground around a bruised birch tree. I thought about how the car had been positioned when we came upon the accident. The windshield and both front windows had been completely broken out. The car had been nose down in the creek and leaning on the near bank.

"I bet she tried to go for help. She could have crawled out of the broken window and left before we found the accident," I suggested.

"That makes sense. It's probably what I would do," Cooper said, the others nodding in agreement.

"We'll start searching right here, where the accident happened," I said, "this side of the brook first since it's closer to town. Everybody spread out along the creek bank, and bark two shorts and a long if you find anything."

We combed through the woods, working our way along systematically in a grid pattern, sniffing for unusual scents or other clues as we walked. We searched all night in the dim light provided by a scant half-moon without success. I called everyone in just before sunrise. "Thanks, everyone, for searching. Even though we didn't find anything, I still think there is a missing dog somewhere in these woods. I'm going to search again this evening after work. Please join me if you can."

I was worried about Ponzie but exhausted from being up all night, so I spent most of the morning catching up on my sleep in Ranger Mike's office. He was busy helping to plan the Acadia Night Sky Festival, the last big event of the season. Scientists and amateur astronomers bring their telescopes up to the top of Cadillac Mountain, and everyone has a great time looking at the heavenly bodies displayed to their best advantage against the dark Acadia night sky.

I have learned, since being assigned to this park, that a dark night sky is a resource that can be protected. The sky is everywhere, of course, but most places where people live, there are lots of lights on all night. Think about it. Parking lots, street lights, car headlights, shopping centers, stadiums, billboards—all that man-made artificial light prevents you from seeing thousands of stars and planets that can be seen in places where the sky is really dark. In Acadia, you can see the Milky Way stretching across the sky, but you don't need a telescope for that—you just look up, and there it is.

When we got home from work, Reggie was waiting in the driveway. "Hi ya, Reggie," Ranger Mike said, giving him a friendly pat on the head.

"I'll be right out," I barked, walking in through the garage with Ranger Mike. I stopped briefly at the toilet in the downstairs bath for a quick drink of water then went straight out the junior ranger door and into the backyard. Reggie walked around to meet me.

"Cooper's not home yet, and Ciara is walking

on a leash with her mom, but I thought we could get an early start searching. There's still an hour or so before sunset."

"Good idea, Reg. Let's go around to the Great Meadow and work our way back to the accident scene from there." The two of us walked along parallel to each other but thirty or so yards apart in order to cover more ground. We walked and sniffed, occasionally pausing at certain large trees and signposts for messages. It's a little hard to explain, but dogs leave messages, kind of like text messages, in places like that—obvious places to whizz, I mean. Like the signpost I had just passed—Jessup Trail. I sniffed it to see who had posted on it that day.

–Cider posted that he was on a walk with his mom and that there was horse poop on the trail.

–Neko posted that he didn't like horse poop but wanted to play chase with Cider later.

–Then Cider posted that he couldn't play chase today, but he could play tomorrow.

–Then Sadie posted, "I thought you said there was horse poop on this trail. I don't see any horse poop."

–Then Corky posted, "Sorry, I ate the horse poop," and that post got 17 likes from other dogs.

But nobody had posted that they were lost or that they had seen a lost dog.

I was becoming concerned. We hadn't found a trace of her and we had searched our way almost back to the accident site. We were only about a quarter of a mile away when I picked up a faint bark. "Arf! Arf–arf–arf!" It was a very excited bark, defensive even, and it sounded like it was coming from a small dog.

Reg is very hard of hearing, so I barked the signal loudly, and he turned my way. I mouthed, "Small dog barking! Come on!"

"Owwooooo!" he howled, and we took off running toward the frantic yelps, barking the signal, two shorts and a long, loudly as we ran.

We splashed through Kebo Brook and ran another hundred yards or so beyond it, bursting out of the woods just above the accident scene. A coyote had cornered Ponzie in front of a large rock formation that protruded out of the ground, and now he was pacing back and forth a few yards away from the frightened dachshund, no doubt waiting for his partner to cut off her escape route.

But the tiny dog stood her ground, challenging the big, bushy-tailed coyote in the quickly fading, post-sunset light. "Back off, you!" She barked, growling as fiercely as possible for a toy-sized breed.

"Ponzie!" I called, skidding to a stop. "Ponzie, are you okay?"

"Thunder! Thank goodness you're here!" she cried with relief.

"Oh, good evening, officer. I was...just asking the lady if she needed any assistance," the coyote interjected, smoothly transforming his demeanor from vicious predator to helpful bystander. But I cut him off right there.

"It's ranger, and this is official park ranger business, coyote. Now clear out of this area."

The coyote gave me a yawn and smacked his lips. "I was just trying to help, ranger," he said innocently. "She was doing all the growling."

"Move along, coyote. I'll take it from here," I said firmly while keeping a neutral tone in my voice. The coyote looked me in the eye. I could tell he was sizing me up, deciding just how far he could push me. Reggie stood tall next to me. I knew he would back me up if it came down to a fight, but the elderly golden was panting hard from the run, and I didn't want anybody to get hurt. It was a very tense situation. I was just thinking, *I need to do something to de-escalate this conflict,* when out of nowhere, Ciara flew past us, launching herself at the coyote like a fluffy blond wrecking ball. She hit him square in the chest with all four paws, rolling him over a half dozen times. *Okay, I* thought, *that'll work too.*

"The ranger said to move along, you big bully!" Ciara boomed, and the coyote tucked his tail and retreated into the night with a couple of whimpering yips. Ciara shook out her fur, each golden tress falling perfectly back into place, and then took a brief moment to smooth down her ears before introducing herself. "Hello, I'm Ciara. You must be Ponzie."

"Oh, thank you! Thank you! I was at the end of my leash!" Ponzie said. "I'm so glad to see you. I need help! I mean, thank you for helping me with the coyote, but I need more help! My parents and I, we had a car accident here a couple of days ago. My mom and dad were hurt, but now they're both gone! I don't know where they are, but wherever they are, they need help! I know this is the right place, but even the car is gone!"

"Wait! Wait!" I interrupted. "We know about the accident. They took your mom and dad to the hospital."

"Oh, thank goodness, I've been so worried." Ponzie sighed with relief.

"We've been looking all over for you, Ponzie. Where have you been? We searched this whole area right after the accident."

"I got lost in the woods," Ponzie said, shaking her head in exasperation. "You see, after the accident, I was really shaken up. It took a few minutes for me to realize what had happened. I mean, the whole car was topsy-turvy. The wheels weren't even touching the ground! My parents weren't moving or talking, and I was afraid they were hurt. So I crawled down to the front of the car. I barked and barked and licked their faces, but I couldn't wake them up. I was scared. I crawled out of the broken window and ran for help, but I couldn't find anyone. I got lost in the woods, and by the time I found my way back, they were gone and so was the car. I didn't know what happened. And then..." She paused a moment. "Come on. I'll show you."

Ponzie led us a short distance into the woods, stopping beside a hollow log. She tugged a sheet of birch bark away from the end of the log, and I peered inside.

"Puppies!"

"Puppies! Let me see!" Ciara squatted on all four paws at the other end of the log. "Awwww! They're so cute!" she squealed. "Congratulations!"

"Yes, congratulations are in order, Ms. Ponzie," Reggie said, taking a quick peek at the puppies.

"Thank you," she said, smiling demurely.

"It was smart to hide them in this log," I observed. "It offers some protection from predators."

"Yes, but when I think about the sweet little nest Mom and I set up for the puppies, right in the nursery..." She blinked back tears.

"Don't cry, sweetie. You and those precious puppies can come home with me," Ciara offered. "I'll help you take care of them."

"I can help too. I live right next door!" I loved the idea of puppies to play with in the neighborhood. "I can bring over some toys."

"That's very kind of you, but I have to stay here. My mom and I saw a video about finding lost dogs the last time we were at the vet's office. It said, if your dog gets lost when you're away from home, leave something with your scent in the last place you saw them. I'm certain my mom will come here to leave something for me as soon as she can because this is the last place she saw me."

Reggie, Ciara, and I looked at each other. "That does makes sense," I said.

"Yes, but who will feed you and fill your

water bowl?" Ciara objected. "Who will play with you and keep you company?"

"I don't know." Ponzie sighed, her head drooping momentarily. "But I know my mom and dad will come here to look for me, and when they do, I have to be here."

She sounded determined, so I knew if we were going to help her, we would have to figure out a way to do it here. "Ranger Mike keeps an extra bag of kibble in the garage. I could bring it out here for you," I suggested, the beginnings of a plan forming in my mind. "And I could babysit the puppies while you go down to the brook to get a drink of water."

"That's good!" Ciara said. "I could come out and keep you company while my mom is at work... and play with the puppies of course."

"Cooper has a day job, and I have two kids at home, but maybe we could take turns coming out at bedtime to see if you need anything," Reggie suggested. "We can help you tuck the little tikes into bed. I'll work out a schedule with Cooper when he gets home."

"That would be wonderful," Ponzie said. "I would love the company, and I am getting pretty hungry."

"Oh! That reminds me. I have something that belongs to you." I bounded quickly back to the creek bank and retrieved the baggie of treats I had taken from the car. "Here, Ponzie, it's your treat bag. I got it from the car before they towed it away."

Ponzie sniffed the bag, savoring the scent. "Mmm...Mom's liver cookies, and I still get a little of my mom's scent too, from the bag. Thank you, Thunder." We heard a faint whimper, and Ponzie peeked inside the log to check on the puppies. "They're starting to stir around a little; I better get back to them. Could one of you cover the end of the log from the outside, please?"

"Sure," I said. I would have had difficulty crawling inside the hollow log, but the miniature dachshund walked into the tiny den without even ducking her head. I covered the end with a chunk of bark, and we camouflaged it with some branches and loose leaves. When we finished, you couldn't even tell the log was hollow. "Come, on guys. We better go," I said. "We'll be back tomorrow with the kibble, Ponzie."

"Night, night, sleep tight!" Ciara whispered, and the search party headed for home.

CHAPTER 13

"I've got it. I've got it," I said to Ciara early the next morning. She was holding the junior ranger door open for me to shove through the bag of kibble Ranger Mike keeps on hand for emergencies. This was an emergency, after all, and I was certainly happy to donate the food to Ponzie and her family. It was just that twenty-five pounds was a lot heavier than I thought it would be, and I was having a little trouble with the logistics.

"Just push it through with your nose," Ciara said for the third time. She was starting to sound a little agitated, but honestly, I was doing my best.

"You know, the bag is twenty-five pounds, and I'm only fifty pounds myself," I said defensively. Putting my shoulder to the bag, I shoved as hard as I could, but I couldn't get any traction on the smooth kitchen floor. My feet kept slipping out from under me. I was running at top speed but going nowhere.

"Going on a picnic?" Spot said from behind me. *That's all I need to make this errand complete—a heckler.* I could hear her cat motor running as she waited for a response. She had the loudest motor in the whole feline world, so how did she keep sneaking up on me like this?

"No, I'm taking this food to a needy dog. She's lost, and she's waiting for her parents to come looking for her. Do you think you could help me push?"

"No, but could you wait a second before you try that again? I want to get Ranger Mike's phone so I can upload a video of this to my YouTube channel."

"Honestly, I don't know why–"

"Humph!" I was cut off by an exasperated Ciara, who grabbed the bag from the outside and pulled it through the door in one smooth motion. I followed.

"Thanks, Ciara. Now give me a minute to catch my breath, and then I can drag the bag through the woods to Ponzie's camp. It's a sturdy bag. I think it will be okay. "

"Oh, for heaven's sake," Ciara said. She picked up the bag and trotted off in the direction of the dachshund family's den. I went back inside to have breakfast with Ranger Mike before work.

It was a two cruise ship day in Bar Harbor. September is the prime month for the gigantic ships to bring thousands of tourists excited to see the beautiful Maine coastline into Bar Harbor. They come ashore to enjoy the quaint charm of our century-old buildings. You see them wide eyed, strolling through the town, taking it all in. But a word of caution: There is so much to see and enjoy in Bar Harbor that tourists tend to inadvertently wander out into the street, camera or phone in hand. You have to be careful not to run them over.

The cruisers also love to sample our town's specialty cuisine: lobsters. Lobsters are to Maine what peanut butter is to jelly, what gravy is to mashed potatoes, and what butter is to bread— except that we save our butter for the lobsters.

Double the cruise ships means double duty. This morning we would lead a guided bicycle tour around the Witch Hole Pond. Ranger Mike stood by the door of the bus that would transport passengers from the town pier to the pond, where the bicycles waited. A lady with a ticket in her hand approached.

"Excuse me, young man. Is this the bus for the lobster bake?

"No, ma'am. This is the bus for the bicycle tour."

"Bicycle tour?"

"Yes, ma'am."

"But my ticket says lobster bake."

"The bus for the lobster bake is over there," Ranger Mike said patiently.

"Over there?"

"Yes, ma'am."

"You're sure?"

"Yes, ma'am."

This scene repeated itself a couple of dozen times until all the seats were filled and the bus pulled out for the short drive to the pond. Along the way, Ranger Mike identified points of interest and answered questions.

"Are we going to an island?" One of the passengers asked. "I thought Acadia was on an island."

"We are on an island."

"No, I mean an island in the ocean—like those." The passenger pointed to the Porcupine Islands.

"We are on an island. You just can't tell it's an island, because you're on it," Ranger Mike explained.

"I can tell an island when I see one. They look like that—with water all around," the man insisted, pointing again to the Porcupines.

"There is water all around. You just can't see all around from here."

"Well, can I change seats then so I can see all around?"

Ranger Mike hesitated for a second. "Sure," he answered.

In the afternoon, we led our last whale watch cruise of the season. There was only one canine passenger aboard, an energetic springer spaniel named Scout. Wide eyed and perky, she was fascinated by everything. It was difficult to get her attention for the mandatory safety lecture.

"Now, Scout, there are only two rules on the whale watch cruise: Rule number one is no number two, and rule number two–"

"I thought you said there is no number two."

"Right, there is no number two, but that's rule number one.

"Okay, no number two is number one. What's number two?"

"Oh, well, you know, it's when you have to... um..."

"No, silly, I know that. I mean, what's rule

number two?"

"Oh, rule number two is don't fall off the boat."

"I've got it," she said, and she bounced off to the bow, put her paws up on the rail, and leaned halfway out over the water while watching for marine life. "I want to see some marine mammals! And some fish! And some lobsters!" she said, her tail wagging so fast it was just a blur.

"Okay," I said, "but I'm not sure you've got rule number two down yet." I kept a close eye on her as the boat skimmed along. Right away, we saw eagles circling over Burnt Porcupine and seals and puffins near the egg rock, and as we left Frenchman Bay, a school of porpoises escorted us partway out to meet the whales.

"Humpbacks off the starboard side," Ranger Mike called out.

"Whales!" Scout yipped excitedly.

"This is your lucky day, Scout. It's very unusual to see whales this close to—hold it! Remember rule number two!"

Scout barked excitedly, "Yoo-hoo! whales!" She bounced up and down, hanging her front paws over the rail to wave at the whales. I grabbed her leash just in case she bounced herself overboard.

With her leash still firmly grasped in my teeth, I looked out to starboard.

"It's Piper!" I barked, waving at her. Piper breached out of the water and came down with a splash. Thanks to Piper and Pearl, the whale watch had become my favorite assignment at Acadia. "That's how a whale waves," I explained to Scout. Piper dove under and swam our way. "Looks like she's coming over to say hello."

The words were barely out of my mouth when her smiling face broke through the water. "Hi, Thunder! Fancy meeting you here, LOL. I know what you're thinking. What are we doing so close to shore, right? Just a little end-of-the-season snack before we migrate south for the winter. The krill off the cliffs here is so tasty. Who's your friend?"

"Piper, this is Scout. She came in on one of the cruise ships."

"I see those cruise ships pass by sometimes. They're positively enormous! And people say whales are big, LOL! Hi, Scout. I hope you're enjoying your trip."

"It's wonderful to meet you, Miss Piper! Can I get a selfie with you? The other spaniels at doggy day care will never believe I met a real humpback whale!"

"How can you get a selfie?" I asked. "You don't have a phone."

"Oh, it's easy. I just pose and look adorable, and my mom takes my picture. You get in the picture too, Thunder." I sat next to Scout and tried to look adorable.

"Get my friend Pearl in the picture too!" Piper said. "Come on, Pearl. Get ready to smile."

"Arf! Arf!" Scout barked. Then she posed herself neatly, adding a little head tilt for that undeniably adorable look, in front of the two broadly smiling whales.

"Oh, that's so cute!" her mom said, clicking the phone in our direction.

Piper and Pearl did their synchronized breaching routine, delighting Scout and the rest of the passengers, as usual. After the performance, Piper said, "Since it's the last whale watch cruise of the season, Pearl and I will be leaving in a couple of weeks for the Caribbean. I'm glad we saw you today, Thunder, so we could say goodbye."

"I'll miss you, girls. I enjoyed working with you both this summer. I hope you'll be back next season."

"You can count on it, Thunder. We love it here at Acadia. Just wait till you see the act we get together for next year's whale watch!" Piper added with her signature giggle. Then she and Pearl swam off, pausing to roll and to wave their flippers one more time.

A couple of weeks later, warm weather and cloudless skies promised perfect conditions for the Night Sky Festival, and almost everyone in town had gone to the mountain-top event. I, however, had opted to stay home that evening. As I believe I've mentioned before, looking through a telescope is not really a dog-friendly activity. I think the stars are pretty, of course, but as a rule, I'm way more interested in things that are close enough for me to smell or chase. Besides, I was due for a little me time. The cruise ship schedule had been keeping me busy most days, and Ponzie's pups kept me busy after work. They were beginning to open their eyes and crawl around, and it was becoming quite a challenge to keep them corralled.

So when Ranger Mike went off to the star party, I settled myself on his comfy chair by the window, resting my chin on the arm so I could look outside. A few minutes later, I saw Reg trot through the yard on his way back from tucking in the pups. He gave me a nod and settled down on his front porch.

"Night, Reg," I barked without getting up.

I must have dozed off soon after that because sometime later, I woke up with a little start. Something seemed wrong, but I couldn't put my paw on it. I jumped down from the chair and looked around the house. Finding nothing unusual inside, I pushed open the junior ranger door and stepped out into the dark back yard. At first, nothing seemed out of the ordinary. I glanced up at the star-filled sky. It really was beautiful, and I was glad that the weather had cooperated for the ranger's star gazing party.

My musings were interrupted when two bucks simultaneously bounded out of the woods. Nothing unusual about that—plenty of deer live in the woods behind the neighborhood. But they had sprinted across the yard without even a nod in my direction, and that was odd behavior. *Hmmm.* I walked over to sniff their tracks and was almost mowed down by a doe and an adolescent fawn as they sprung across the yard. "Hey, watch it," I yelped, but they didn't even slow down. I heard more rustling in the woods. I couldn't see anything, but my nose told me it was a flock of turkeys.

What's got everyone so excited? I lifted my nose to the air and took a deep sniff. Smoke! It could be a campfire, or it could be trouble. I analyzed the composition carefully: dried leaves, birch bark, wood, but not firewood, green wood—like living trees! "The woods are on fire!"

Fire can be a very scary thing on an island, especially if you've ever heard about the big fire of 1947, and trust me on this, everyone has heard about it. The huge fire burned through the park and across the island, and it only narrowly missed burning the whole town to the ground.

I dove back through the junior ranger door. "Spot! Wake up, Spot. The woods are on fire!" I bellowed through the house. How did I know Spot was asleep? Easy—she's always asleep. She slinked through the cat flap that led to her private lair in the basement.

"What's the big emergency?" she demanded.

"Sniff for yourself," I called out. "I've got to report this." I made a beeline to Reggie's house next door. The neighborhood was almost empty, but Reggie had told me his whole family was home sick with a cold. I found him asleep on the front porch, and I gave him a little nudge. Startled, the old veteran jerked awake and looked at me with a bit of annoyance. He started to speak, but I pointed to my nose and mouthed the word "fire." He sniffed the air and struggled to his feet.

"That's a green wood fire," he exclaimed and then carefully tested the air again. "It's not far away, no more than a couple of miles. "We've got to alert the neighborhood!" he barked with alarm. "And I have to get my family out of the house. They're all asleep upstairs!"

"You get your family. I'll warn the neighbors," I said. Reggie dashed into the house, and I launched myself down the driveway at full speed. *I have to warn everyone in a hurry,* I thought. *I need help fast. No! I need fast help!* I only knew one dog who could run as fast as I could, so I bolted across the street to Cooper's front yard. "Arf–arf–arrrrrrf! Arf–arf–arrrrrf!"

A few seconds later, Cooper came barreling out of the house. "What's the deal, Thunder? What's the alarm about?"

"Fire! In the woods. I need help barking up the neighborhood!" I explained quickly. "You go that way, and I'll go this way!"

"I'm on it!" he yelped, and he tore off toward the village.

I skirted the south edge of town that borders the park, signal barking "Fire!" as loudly as I could until other dogs began responding. Then I circled back around to meet Reggie and Cooper in Reggie's front yard.

Reggie had rounded up his family, and he was calmly barking instructions for them to evacuate the island. Reggie turned to tell me something, but he didn't get a chance because his dad snapped a leash on his collar and said, "Come on Reg. Let's get moving."

"I've got to look after them," Reggie said. "They're afraid to go without me."

"Don't worry. We've got this," I assured him as Cooper appeared by my side, panting from his Paul Revere-like gallop through town.

Reggie got into the Subaru with his family. The engine started, and as the car began rolling down the driveway, Reggie's head appeared out of the back window. "Thunder," he barked, "the puppies! Don't forget the puppies!"

"Right," I yelped. I looked at Cooper. He nodded, signaling me that he was prepared to do whatever needed to be done. We turned toward the woods and saw Ciara running down the driveway next door. "Come on, Cooper," I barked, and we bounded over to intercept Ciara.

"Where's the fire?" she demanded, not waiting for an answer but lifting her nose to sniff the air for herself.

"Ponzie will need help moving the puppies," I said. "Can you help us move them?"

"Of course. Let's go," she responded, but then she added, "Wait, how many puppies are there? It never occurred to me to count them. I just played with them."

"Yeah," Cooper added, "can we carry them all?"

"I don't know," I lamented. "We didn't study math at the Canine Academy, only sit and stay."

"I know math," a voice behind us purred coolly. "I've seen those puppies, and there are either seven or twelve of them," Spot said with authority. "Either way, you three can't carry them all. You need one more dog."

"We don't have time to get another dog. Will you help us carry one of the puppies?" I implored.

"Yes, please, Spot," Ciara added. "They're very small, not too heavy."

"Of course I would like to help, but I have to rescue my toy rodent collection. If the fire gets too close, they'll all smell like smoke instead of catnip."

"Please, Spot!" I pleaded. "Ranger Mike will get you more stuffies, I'm sure of it." *Of course he will*, I thought. *Ranger Mike is constantly bringing home treats and toys for that feline. He brought her a new toy, covered with real feathers, just last week! Hello, I'm a bird dog. Don't you think I might like to have a new feather toy to play with? Wait! Thunder, focus!* I told myself.

Spot dropped the stuffed mouse she was carrying outside the junior ranger door and scurried back inside to rescue more of her toys.

"Come on," I said. "We'll figure something out."

We ran through the woods to Ponzie's camp and found her carefully trying to herd the rambunctious puppies away from the path of the fire. "We're here to help you move the puppies," I yelped.

We could hear the fire crackle and see its red glow in the distance just beyond the ridge. It was moving closer with every passing second. "We have to move fast," I advised. "We don't have enough dogs to carry all the puppies, so let's set up some kind of relay system to get them out as quickly as possible," I suggested, coming up with a plan on the fly.

"Take it easy. I'm here," Spot meowed loudly, coming up the trail just behind us.

"Thanks for helping, Spot," I said gratefully.

"You owe me for this, bird dog," she hissed.

"Everyone grab a puppy, and let's get out of these woods before we all get caught in the fire," I ordered. I reached down and picked up the smallest puppy, the runt of the tiny litter. "It's okay, pup. You're safe," I told her, and I passed her to Spot. Ponzie picked up another of the pups and followed Spot through the woods.

"Take a puppy, and stick close to Spot and Ponzie," I told Cooper. "Sometimes hawks and owls hunt in the path of a fire. Small animals trying to escape can become an all-you-can-eat buffet for birds of prey."

"Right," he chirped. He grabbed a puppy and took off after them.

Ciara looked into my eyes. "You're so cool in a crisis," she said, "so commanding, so brave." She leaned toward me and licked my face with kisses. Then she quickly picked up a puppy and ran after the others.

I smiled from ear to ear, and my face started to feel hot, but I was not sure if it was from the kisses or the fire. *I better get the last pup out of here,* I thought, and I looked down—*Nooooo! There's two of them!* "Spot!" I yelled in frustration. *That cat doesn't know math any more than I do, but dwelling on that isn't going to help me now. I need a plan.* I ran through my options.

I could try to carry both puppies at the same time. A brief experiment quickly told me this option was not possible. I would carefully pick up one puppy, but when I tried to pick up the other one, the first pup easily wiggled out of my grip.

I tried to herd them toward town, but that was also ineffective. They crawled off in any and every direction randomly, and I spent more time getting them back on the trail than moving them away from the fire.

I finally settled on a leap frog technique. I picked up one pup, ran him up the trail thirty feet or so, dropped him, ran back to get the other one, moved him thirty feet or so past the first one, and so on. It was slow going. Thick smoke was closing in around us, and I could feel the hot breeze generated by the fire. I knew it was catching up to us, but I couldn't come up with a better option. I just knew I had to keep moving. I developed a bit of a rhythm: pup one–pup two–pup one–pup two.

Suddenly, I heard a loud shrieking call above the sound of the fire. "Kahhhhhhhh, kak–kak–kak–kak."

I looked up and saw a broad pair of wings flanking a sharp beak coming right at me. I huddled protectively over pup one and pup two. "I'm warning you. These pups are off limits!" I said with all the authority I could muster. But to my surprise, the outstretched talons did not reach for the pups but came lightly to rest on a big stump just off the trail. As the bird folded his mottled gray and tan wings, I noticed the slight pattern difference in the feathers of the left wing tip. "Perrot!" I exclaimed. "Perrot, what are you doing here?"

"Thun-dare, you seem to be in a bit of trouble, my friend," he pointed out.

"I have to get these puppies away from the fire," I said urgently, "and safely to the town pier. I promised their mother."

"Let me help you, Thun-dare. I can fly one of those puppies out for you in no time; then you can run with the other one."

"But Perrot, I know that raptors sometimes target small mammals fleeing a fire. No, these pups are my responsibility."

"You saved my life, Thun-dare, and you saved my family. You can trust me. I give you my word of honor that I will deliver that puppy safely to the town pier," he said solemnly. "Besides, I don't think you're going to make it without my help," he added as another loud boom signaled the progress of the fire. "Trust me. You're limited by a ground-level perspective. I've seen the fire from the air."

I hesitated only a moment. "Okay, on your word of honor," and I relinquished one of the pups.

Perrot carefully picked him up. "I shall deliver him to his mother safe and sound. You can count on me, Thun-dare," he assured me, and he flapped away on his powerful wings.

"Come on, pup!" I hollered over the noise of the approaching fire. "Let's get out of here!" I grabbed him by the scruff and started to run. With only one pup to move, I made it quickly back to the outskirts of town, where I passed the Bar Harbor Fire Department speeding toward the fire. Halfway to the town pier, I met Cooper coming back to see if I needed help.

"Dude! Your friend Perrot showed up at the pier with one of the puppies. I thought you might be in trouble, so I was coming back to help," Cooper panted.

I put my puppy down for a second. "I need to study math," I said. "That's the only trouble now. Come on. Let's get this little guy back to Ponzie and the rest of the litter."

Cooper led me straight to Ponzie, where Spot was helping to keep the puppies corralled. I placed the last puppy with the others.

The pier was crowded, and smoke mixed with

the fog in the air, making it difficult to see. Nobody panicked, but it was a little chaotic as people that had been at the star party looked to reunite with those that had been at home when the fire broke out.

"Look, there's Reggie," Cooper said. "I'll go let him know the puppies are safe."

"I'm going to find Ciara," I said, and we walked off in opposite directions.

I saw Ciara in the crowd and headed over to tell her I had delivered the last puppy safely, but as soon as her mom saw me, she pulled out her phone. "I see him, Commander Coop. He's here on the town pier with me. Don't worry. I'll keep him here till they arrive." She put the phone away and said, "Come here, Cooper. The commander has been looking all over for you."

"I'm not Cooper," I protested. "I'm Thunder." But she had no idea what I was saying, and she slipped a spare leash around my neck. I was stuck.

Ciara shook her head. "My mom is so cute," she said, "but smart? Let's just say I don't know how she would get along without me."

"No big deal," I said. "I wanted to stay here with you anyway, Ciara."

Meanwhile, over on the beach, Reggie's dad

was on the phone with Ranger Mike. "I see him, Ranger Mike. Don't worry. He'll be safe with us." He put a leash on Cooper and said, "Come on, Thunder. You stay here with us while Ranger Mike is busy helping put out the fire."

"But I'm Cooper. Thunder is over there," he tried to explain, but to Reggie's dad, one Vizsla looks just like another.

Reggie shook his head. "Don't worry. You two can just switch out when we get home. I don't know why humans even have noses; they can't smell a thing."

I looked over at Cooper down the beach a hundred yards or so with Reggie's dad. He jiggled the leash and shrugged. I shrugged too. I mean, what could we do? They would figure it out eventually. After all, it was a bit funny that they couldn't tell us apart.

It was funny, that is, until the Coast Guard van pulled up to the pier. Two midshipmen in uniform stepped out and walked purposefully straight toward me. As they approached, I could feel my tail involuntarily creeping farther and farther between my legs, and my ears flattening out on the back of my head. *What's going on here? Am I in some kind of trouble? Is it illegal to use a falcon to transport a puppy? Did someone find out I pooped in the park four times one day when Ranger Mike only had three poop bags?*

I could hear Cooper barking loudly on the beach. "Over here, guys!" he howled. "Arr, arr, arr, are you kidding me? Over here!" He strained frantically at the leash, yelping at the top of his lungs.

But the uniforms made a beeline straight to me and asked Ciara's mom, "Is this Canine Cooper?"

"Yes," she assured them, "the commander told me you'd be coming for him."

"Thank you, ma'am," one of them responded.

The other one took the leash. "Come on, Cooper. Come on, boy. It's time to go to work!" he said, giving the leash a slight tug.

To say I was reluctant to accompany them is quite an understatement. I'm happy to serve my country; don't get me wrong. It's just that I like to know *what* I'm going to do to serve my country, you understand, and I had no idea what was going on at all. I planted my front paws on the boards and sat my behind down.

"He must be upset about the fire and all the commotion," the other uniform surmised. "Don't worry, Cooper. The fire department has the fire under control. It was close, but they stopped it before it got into town." Then he picked me up and carried me to the van.

Cooper was still barking his head off, but when he saw us get into the van, he realized nobody understood and finally gave up in frustration. My face was plastered to the window as the van pulled away from the pier. Our eyes met, and Cooper barked, "Don't worry, Thunder. It's probably just a drill."

CHAPTER 14

"That's all I know," I said to the Lab. "I don't even know what kind of a drill. I thought he was the unit mascot or something. Maybe you can tell me what I'm doing here. You probably know more about it than I do," I pointed out.

He ignored my comment and eyed me suspiciously. "So you expect me to believe that this is a simple case of mistaken identity? Not likely. How do I know you're not a spy attempting to steal top secret information—information vital to the security of the United States of America? Valuable information that you could sell or trade—for dog biscuits!"

My ears pricked up. "Wh–wh–what are you talking about?" I stammered. "I would never do anything like that!"

"Oh really..." He drew the last word out, watching me sweat, and then he blurted his accusation. "Not even for Hungary? Your native land? Because you're not just a Vizsla are you? You're a Hungarian Vizsla!"

"What? No! Wait, yes, but–but–but," I blustered. Then I got a grip on myself. "Okay, yes, I'm a Hungarian Vizsla—but we're *all* Hungarian Vizslas! Even Cooper! That doesn't mean I'm Hungarian. I've never even been to Hungary! I'm from Texas, the Lone Star State! I'm strictly red, white, and blue! Except for the white and blue, of course, because I'm all red."

"I don't know..." he said skeptically.

"Come on, I'm no spy—I'm a junior park ranger! They don't give those badges to just anybody, you know!"

"Well, I suppose I could take you on as a trainee, under the circumstances. Today's test is critical. The fate of the entire program may rest on the results of this alpha-level, high-security breach detection simulation."

"Wow! That sounds official!" My eyes widened, and my ears pricked. I leaned in to ensure I heard every word.

"Yes, but I'm warning you, it could be dangerous," he cautioned.

"Danger is my middle name...err...more or less," I qualified my statement because I wanted to be completely truthful. My middle name is actually Haleakala. It's Hawaiian, but in my defense, I don't really know what it means. For all I know, Haleakala does mean danger.

"Okay, trainee, my name is Rocco. I'm the senior canine and team captain. Before I read you in on this op, let me remind you that this information is top secret. You can't tell anyone what I'm about to tell you."

"You can count on me!" I said, acknowledging his words by pantomiming locking my lips shut and throwing away the key. "My lips are sealed."

"Okay, trainee, our mission is to detect bombs and unauthorized ordinance that terrorists or other criminals may be attempting to bring into the country through harbors and sea ports. You may be a junior park ranger most days, but today you're in the U.S. Coast Guard."

"Yes, sir," I responded, saluting with my paw. "How do we detect bombs?"

"We use the most sophisticated bomb detection technology currently available to military and civilian organizations—our noses." He pointed to his snout with his paw. "How's your nose, son?" he asked.

"I've got a good nose, sir," I assured him, pointing to my own nose. "Solid."

"Good," he said. "Now, the procedure is very

complicated. We differentiate between at least a dozen highly complex mixtures of scents that may be found in various explosive compounds. The amounts and exact mixtures of these components may vary depending on the origin of the device, so it is vital to identify any of the key ingredients when the scent is detected."

I nodded.

"It takes years of rigorous training for a bomb detection canine to learn all of the various scent mixtures that could indicate the presence of explosives. Normally I would never be able to teach you enough to detect a bomb in the time we have before the drill is scheduled to begin, but today we've caught a lucky break because Canine Cooper is a specialist."

I looked at him intensely. "A specialist?" I repeated.

"That's right. His job is to look for one specific type of bomb. Even though the concentration of chemicals may vary, each bomb of this type will have a distinct scent signature underlying the compound. All you have to do is be able to detect that one scent."

I nodded. "One distinct scent signature." I was trying to appear calm, but knowing how complicated the training was and how the whole program was riding on the performance of my nose, the stress was starting to get to me. I was vibrating with nervous energy and hanging on Rocco's every word. Inside my head, self-doubt wrestled with my confidence, threatening to come out of my mouth audibly so I would have no choice but to hear it with my own ears. *How good is my nose really? What if I fail?* But I subdued my insecurities long enough to squeak out, "Yes, sir," and he continued.

"This scent signature has a very close analog that is commonly found in nature. I have never smelled it myself, but I am told by experts that these bombs smell almost exactly like a skunk. Son, have you ever smelled skunk spray?"

I felt my whole body relax. "Have I ever smelled skunk spray?" I repeated incredulously. "You mean, the thing I have to find, the thing that will determine the success or failure of this whole alpha-level drill, and the future of the entire Coast Guard Canine Ordinance Detection program, smells like a skunk?" I almost laughed with relief. That was one smell I would never forget after being sprayed in the face twice by my now good friend Seymour the skunk, on my last assignment in Vicksburg.

"Yes," he said. With a stern look on his face,

he stared at me intently and asked, "Can you do it, son?"

I held up my paw to stop the discourse. "Oh, I got this," I told him with assurance. "You can relax, sir. If it's skunk scent you need detected, I'm your canine. I'm an expert on that particular scent signature."

"That's good. Good dog," he barked. "Now, when you find the bomb, you sit down in front of it. That's how you signal to your human partner that you've found something."

"Yes, sir, sit in front of it. I got it, sir," I acknowledged.

"These tests are usually out on a container ship or a barge to simulate real conditions. We'll fly out on a helicopter to meet the ship," the Lab informed me while we waited for our human partners to return.

"Cool! I always wanted to ride in a helicopter," I said. "How does it land on the ship?"

"Oh, it doesn't land on the ship. We slide down on ropes."

"Ropes! But–but–but–" Just then the door open, and our human partners breezed back in.

"Time to gear up, boys. Chopper is here," one of them announced.

CHAPTER 15

I had learned from Rocco that my partner's name was Bates and his partner was Conway. Bates led me into the locker room, where he helped me into a special harness with lots of buckles and a steel link attached on the back. He strapped headphones over my ears to protect them from the loud noise of the helicopter then put reflective mirror-lensed goggles that were specially designed for dogs over my eyes. I caught a glimpse of myself in the locker room mirror. I looked cool. Bates gave me a thumbs-up.

"Woof," I said, and I gave him a paw bump. *That's right,* I thought. *We've got swagger.* I was feeling it as Bates and I rejoined Rocco and his partner outside the locker room and the four of us strutted across the tarmac to the helicopter and climbed inside.

A few minutes later, out over open ocean, it wasn't as easy to maintain my bravado. I was thinking about what Rocco had said about sliding down to the ship on ropes. I've got substantial, all-terrain paws that will take me just about anywhere, but I didn't see how I could use them to slide down a rope. *I hope they remember I don't have thumbs.* I looked over at Rocco. He seemed calm and unconcerned about our upcoming descent. I decided to follow his lead on that for the time being—after all, he was the team leader; it was his job to worry, not mine—so I turned my attention to the scenery.

The sun was poised to break over the horizon any minute now, and the sky was bathed with the soft, pink light of predawn. The ocean below appeared pink as well; its mirror surface was undisturbed by any movement, perfectly reflecting the sky. I was still captivated by the peaceful scene when I detected movement off to the left and turned my attention to the source. It was two whales in the water below. The pair was swimming in perfect sync, each gracefully breaching at the same time with a big splash, both flukes simultaneously disappearing under the water, followed by twin spouts as they surfaced. *It must be Piper and Pearl,* I realized, *beginning their migration to the Caribbean. I'll have to tell them next summer I saw them practicing from a helicopter. They'll flip!*

Every minute that passed brought dawn closer and saturated the sky with even darker pink light, and by the time the sun breached the horizon, the sky could only be described as red. "Red sky in morning, sailor take warning," Bates remarked, repeating my thought out loud.

"That's just an old superstition," Conway responded. "Come on. Let's get ready. I can see the ship up ahead."

I could see the ship up ahead too. It was gigantic! The decks were covered with hundreds of colorful containers, each one the size of a semi-truck. "We're supposed to search all that?" I asked Rocco.

"Is there a problem, trainee?" he barked. "I thought you said you have a good nose."

"No problem, sir," I responded.

Bates and Conway stood up and began to thread lines through pulleys attached to the ceiling just inside the door of the helicopter. They tied steel clamps onto the lines with special knots and tested their strength. When they were satisfied with the rigging, Bates attached one of the steel carabiners to a harness; then he put the harness on, double checking each buckle as he snapped them shut. Then he attached one last carabiner to the front of the harness and said, "Come, Cooper."

Nobody moved. Rocco cleared his throat. "He means you, Thunder," he mumbled.

"Oh, yes, sure," I acknowledged somewhat reluctantly as I inched a few steps closer to Bates. Bates tugged at all my buckles to make sure they were secure; then he snapped the carabiner onto the steel ring on my harness.

"Let's go," he said.

The next thing I knew, we were hanging out over the ocean, suspended by our harnesses outside the helicopter. I could feel panic stirring around in my stomach, but I remembered that Cooper and Rocco were counting on me. I took a deep breath and subdued my fear. The stern of the huge vessel was directly beneath us now. Bates was holding me more or less in his lap as the winch began to let out line, and we descended toward the deck. The wind was blowing us around some, but not too much, and we were on the deck in no time.

Bates quickly knelt down and detached the steel carabiner from my harness. "Stay," he said. He needn't have bothered; I wasn't going anywhere. The deck was loud. There were unfamiliar noises coming from every direction, and we were surrounded by huge towers of cargo containers that were even bigger than they appeared to be from the air. There were about a dozen people watching our every move. Some of them were from the crew, and some of them were Coast Guard evaluators who had come to monitor the test.

I was inundated with unfamiliar smells, mostly similar to what I think of as mechanical smells, like from a truck engine or a garage but much, much stronger. No wonder the test was conducted on a real ship. It would be almost impossible to recreate this level of sensory chaos in a controlled environment. This test was going to be quite a challenge.

Rocco and his partner rode down quickly from the chopper and joined us on deck. Rocco had told me that speed was a factor in the test, so after brief instructions from the   captain, the official timekeeper said, "Begin," and started his stop watch.

"Seek!" Bates ordered, and we were off. He led me down one row of containers after another while I sniffed along the bottom of each one, searching for the familiar scent of skunk musk. It wasn't hard to do. Even though I was surrounded by strong smells, my sensitive nose sorted them out and reduced them to their component parts. A lot of the training that canine and human bomb detection personnel receive is about how to communicate with each other. Plenty of dogs could go in on the first day and pick out any smell a human asked for if that person could ask for it

in a language the dog could understand. Rocco and I didn't have to overcome the language gap; he explained it to me dog to dog.

We had been working for the better part of an hour when I caught a whiff of a non-mechanical-related odor that strongly reminded me of skunk musk. It was coming from inside—no, from underneath one of the containers. I doubled back to re-sniff the area, and Bates followed. Carefully, I zeroed in on the familiar scent, sniffing for the highest concentration. Sniff...sniff... *This is it,* I determined. I carefully analyzed the scent, dissecting it within my powerful nose. *Yep, I'm sure this is it.* I sat down right on the spot, and I looked up at Bates. Bates blew a whistle, and the Coast Guard monitors hurried over to us.

"Congratulations, Bates and Cooper. You have identified the correct container well within the time limit. Good work, and welcome to the team!" the captain exclaimed with a smile, shaking Bates's hand and patting me on the head.

"Good boy, Cooper!" Bates said with enthusiasm. I didn't really know if Cooper was a kisser, but I planted a big one on Bates's face as he leaned in to congratulate me. I was pretty happy to have passed even though technically it was Cooper who had passed.

We ate lunch with the crew, and the cook served Rocco and me cheeseburgers he made special for us with lots of ketchup and no pickles and onions. They were so delicious that I was still licking my lips as Bates and I walked out of the mess room and back up to the deck.

"This way, Cooper, uh, I mean Thunder. We're taking the launch back to the station with the captain and the rest of the team," Rocco explained. "The chopper is taking the observers back to Boston."

"Too bad. I could get used to riding in that chopper," I said. The crew disengaged our patrol boat from the huge cargo ship and turned for the trip back to Mount Desert Island. Rocco and I settled ourselves in a sunny corner at the stern of the vessel. I could feel a nap coming on. After all, it was late afternoon, and I had been up all night.

"Ahem." Rocco cleared his throat. "I just want to say, trainee, you did very well on that test. I almost forgot that you weren't Cooper myself for a minute there. So good boy!"

"Thank you, sir," I said. Even though I had just met Rocco that morning, I knew he was a pro, and his praise meant a lot to me.

"Yes, well, don't let it go to your head," Rocco

grumbled, flopping down on his side for a nap. I curled up too and dozed off with a smile on my face.

"See, I told you, 'Red sky in morning, sailor take warning.' This storm is going to be a doozy," I heard Bates saying, and I opened one eye to peek at the sky. Dark clouds had taken over in the hour I had been asleep, and they were growing thicker by the moment. Reflecting the sky, the water appeared dramatically different too, dark and forbidding.

"What's our ETA, skipper?" Conway asked. "Do you think we can beat this storm?"

"I don't know, but we're sure going to try. We're coming up on Great Duck Island, and that means we're still over an hour out. Looks like we might get wet."

"Look!" Bates was pointing toward the distant island on our starboard horizon. "A humpback whale."

I remembered seeing Pearl and Piper from the helo that morning. *I bet it's them,* I thought, and I jumped up to take a look. "That's Piper. I'd know her fluke anywhere. She's a friend of mine," I explained to Rocco, who was standing next to me at the rail. "I work with her on my real job as a junior park ranger."

"Right, I almost forgot you have a job of your own."

"Looks like she's coming this way. She's very friendly." But as I watched, I could tell there was something odd about her behavior. *She can't know I'm on board. This is a Coast Guard vessel. Still, it looks like she's trying to get our attention.* Bates had noticed it too.

"Skipper, I know it sounds crazy, but I think that whale is trying to intercept us," Bates said incredulously, watching her through his binoculars.

"Help! Help!" Piper shouted as best she could while swimming at top speed. Coughing and sputtering between words, she approached within a few yards of the boat, attempting to match our speed as she swam alongside us. "Help! Please, my friend needs help!"

"Piper!" I barked. "Piper, what's wrong?"

"Thunder! Thunder, Pearl needs help! She's caught in fishing gear. It's wrapped all around her fluke, and she can't swim! She's trapped!" Piper was in a panic, and rightfully so. It would be almost impossible for a whale to untangle itself from lines wrapped around its fluke. The lines are very difficult to break, and trying to break them would likely result in a serious skin injury and possibly a slow, painful death from infection.

"Where is she? I can't see her," I asked urgently.

"She's around the far side of this island. Thunder, you've got to do something!"

"Skipper, before the Coast Guard, I interned with Allied Whale through the College of the Atlantic. This is very unusual whale behavior," Bates said with concern. We couldn't see Pearl from where we were, and I knew the humans couldn't possibly understand what Piper had told me, but Bates knew enough about whales to be curious. Maybe he could convince the skipper to investigate. I gave him the whining sad eye.

"Unh–unh–unh," I whined urgently.

"Sir, I really think something is wrong," Bates urged again.

"Bates, I don't know what you're talking about, but I do know we don't have time for a sightseeing whale watch expedition today. Look at those clouds. The wind is blowing at 20 knots, and we're a long way from the harbor."

"Yes, sir," Bates said.

"Full ahead, helmsman," the skipper ordered, and the boat began to move away quickly.

"Thunder! Please don't leave. Do something!" Piper pleaded.

Shakily, I put my paws on the rail.

"What are you doing, trainee?" Rocco barked with alarm. "Stand down, trainee. Stand down!"

"Sorry, Rocco. This is park ranger business." I took a deep breath—*Cooper, I hope they really like you*—and I jumped.

CHAPTER 16

I bobbed up in the dark gray water and started swimming as fast as I could, following Piper toward the island. I barely even noticed the frigid temperature of the water. Behind me, I heard Bates shout from the stern of the boat. "Man overboard! Man overboard! No, dog overboard!" In the background, a bell clanked frantically, accompanied by the loud whoop, whoop, whoop of the patrol boat's alarm.

"Hard about," the skipper ordered. The boat turned in a wide sweeping arc and headed after me. I didn't look back; I kept up my determined dog paddle, intent on covering as much distance as possible in the time I had. I had to make it far enough that Bates and the others on board would have a clear line of sight to the back side of the island where Pearl was tethered.

Piper swam ahead of me. "This way, Thunder," she called out. The boat was right on top of me now. Just a few more meters...

"Gotcha!" Bates said, scooping me out of the water with a long-handled net. Conway helped him haul me back into the boat.

"Woof–woof–woof," I barked as soon as I had all four paws on deck. I rushed up to the bow and executed a perfect point in the direction Piper had led me. They all stared at me.

"What's the matter with that canine, Bates? Can't you get him under control?" the captain demanded.

"Woof!" I barked again and gave another perfect point. Nothing! *Come on! What's the problem, guys? When I point, you don't look at me—you look at where I'm pointing!*

Out in the distance, Piper breached, lifting her entire body out of the water. "Over here!" she shouted, lobbing her tail on the water to get their attention.

Bates looked out at Piper, then back at me, then at Piper. He grabbed his binoculars and scanned the horizon. "Sir, it's another whale, and it looks like it's in distress!"

In spite of the storm, the captain turned the boat toward the anxious animal. As we approached, he joined us on deck. "I radioed NOAA that we have a humpback in imminent danger," he said. "They're standing by, ready to respond as soon as the storm clears, but there's a long line of fronts moving through. It's likely to be morning before they can make it."

"Sir, the water is so shallow here that she could get washed up on the beach in the storm. Let me get close enough to take a look at the lines." Bates said. "I have training in marine mammal rescue."

The skipper glanced at the sky. Lightning broke in the clouds at the leading edge of the storm, followed by low, rumbling thunder. I've never been afraid of thunder, perhaps a side benefit of being named after the phenomenon, but lightning and thunder out on the open sea was a little disconcerting. None the less, I was steadfast in my determination to help Pearl. The look on Bates's face showed he shared my resolve. I stood by his side on the deck, waiting for word from the captain.

"Okay, Bates, take the Zodiac. But be careful, and stay out of the water. Conway, you go with him."

Bates took a sharp knife from its sheath and strapped it securely to the end of the boat pole. Then he and Conway put on their helmets and floatation gear and climbed down into the raft. The high sea tossed the flimsy orange craft, but the guys made steady progress.

"Pearl," I barked, "my friend Bates is coming to cut you loose. Be careful of the raft, Pearl. Try not to flip it."

"Thunder, I'm scared! I can't swim away!"

"I know, Pearl. They're coming right now. Just hold on a few more minutes."

Bates moved the raft into position. "It's a simple case, sir. A single line is wrapped around the fluke and anchored to something heavy below the surface. I don't know what's down there, but whatever it is, it's a lot heavier than a lobster trap." Bates took the long-handled knife and carefully cut the line away. "There you go, Ms. Humpback. You're free!"

Tentatively, Pearl wiggled her fins and moved several meters forward. "I can swim! I'm free!" She dove under the water and popped up on the other side of the boat, and the whole crew cheered.

"Thank you, Thunder, thank you! That was the scariest thing that's ever happened to me. You can't imagine how terrifying it is for a whale not to be able to swim," she said.

"Pearl, that's the most I've heard you say all summer," I said. Pearl grinned and turned fluke up before swimming out to meet Piper.

"Thunder, you're the best junior park ranger ever!" Piper called.

I blushed. "Bye, girls. Be careful. It's a long way to the West Indies. See you next year!"

"See you on the whale watch," they called out together, and they water and swam off to the south.

"Good work, guys," the skipper said when Bates and Conway climbed back on board. "Now stow that raft, and let's get out of here. This storm's not going to hold off much longer."

The captain turned our boat for home, and I watched the girls swim away for as long as I could see them. Rocco walked over to join me at the rail. "That was good work, trainee. You're a good dog. If you ever want to join the Coast Guard for real, I'd be happy to put in a good word for you with the station commander."

"I appreciate that, Rocco, but I've still got a lot to learn about the parks. Besides, my partner, Ranger Mike, would be lost without me."

"I certainly understand. I'm not sure Conway could find his way home without me." We both chuckled. Then the air temperature dropped distinctly as the clouds caught up to the boat and poured rain down on us. Not a little rain either—it seemed to be coming in from all sides at once.

Cold and wet, I found Bates and sat down beside him. Both wet and shivering in the rain, we looked at each other. "Totally worth it, buddy," Bates said with a smile.

"Totally," I barked.

When the boat pulled into Southwest Harbor later that night, Bates dried me off with a towel and drove me home. He stopped in front of Cooper's house of course, but until then, I had almost forgotten about the mix-up.

"Exciting day today, Cooper. You accomplished a lot. You passed your certification test and saved that whale." I licked his face. "I know I helped actually cut the lines, but we would never have seen her if you hadn't jumped in. I don't know how you knew a whale was in trouble, but that was really brave. I'm recommending you for a commendation." I licked his face again. "I'll tell you something else...I think that whale was trying to say thank you."

"Woof," I agreed.

He let me out of the van, and I trotted up to Cooper's front door, waited till Bates was out of sight, then hauled it across the street to my house, where Cooper met me outside the junior ranger door, a look of supreme expectation on his rusty red face. "You passed," I said.

"Booya!" he exclaimed. "I don't know how to thank you, dude! I'm sorry it worked out this way. I've been looking forward to that test for weeks now."

"It's just as well. I ran into some friends of mine who were in trouble on the way back, and your partner, Bates, helped them out for me. He's a good guy. I liked him."

"Yeah, Bates is a great partner." Cooper nodded. "Well, I better get home. One of us should report to the commander."

"Right. Night, buddy," I said. "Oh, and, Cooper…if anyone gives you a commendation, just smile and say thank you."

"Sure thing, dude." Cooper trotted off, and I went inside.

"In for the night, buddy?" Ranger Mike said, giving me a pat on the head. "You look tired, pal." As far as he was concerned, I'd just been hanging out in the yard. I gave him a few wags and walked straight to my bed. I'd make it up to him tomorrow. Right now I was exhausted. I curled up in my bed and fell right to sleep.

The next morning, I woke up feeling great about all I had accomplished. I came downstairs, and Ranger Mike poured out a big bowl of kibble for me. I was starving, and I dug in with gusto. After breakfast, I ran out to fetch the Sunday paper, and a car pulled into the driveway. While I alerted Ranger Mike that we had company, a man pulled a huge cellophane-covered basket tied with a big red bow out of the back seat. It was so big that he could hardly carry it up to the porch, where Ranger Mike and I waited.

"Delivery for Spot," the driver said, placing the basket on the porch and handing Ranger Mike an iPad to sign. The basket smelled like catnip and was full of the sparkly, fluffy kinds of toys that cats like to play with. Ranger Mike pulled out a bag of stinky treats that was made out of snails or something gross.

"Spot? Spot, my cat?" Ranger Mike asked skeptically.

"That's what the order says." The driver smiled and shrugged his shoulders.

"Who would have sent Spot a gift?" Ranger Mike carried the basket inside. "Here kitty, kitty," he called, taking the newspaper from my mouth.

He opened it and read out loud, "Hero Cat Saves Litter of Puppies! Spot, you're a hero!"

He dropped the paper and picked her up. On the front page, I saw a big picture of Spot standing over Ponzie and the puppies on the beach after the fire. Someone must have taken it after the Coast Guard picked me up. *Well, that just figures, doesn't it?* I thought. She sneered down at me from Ranger Mike's arms. "Who's a big hero, kitty? Who's the bravest kitty in the world to save those puppies?"

Seriously? She's getting a gift basket and all the credit! Come on! I rolled my eyes and sniffed the basket again. Not a single dog treat or toy officially approved for canine use. I just sat there shaking my head while Ranger Mike helped her try out all those new toys. After a few minutes, I heard Ciara barking for me to come outside.

"Did you see the paper this morning? They're calling Spot a hero," I complained. "They didn't even mention us at all."

"Oh, who cares," Ciara said. "Ponzie and the pups are okay, and that's all that matters. Now come with me. I have a surprise that will cheer you right up." I followed Ciara over to her yard, where a strange car was parked in the driveway. We walked up on the porch and peered in through the screen door.

"Good morning, Thunder" Ciara's mom opened the door for us to come inside, where two people, one with his leg in a cast, and the other holding the tiniest human I had ever seen, were sitting on the floor playing with the puppies. The same puppies that just forty-eight hours ago, my friends and I had carried to safety ahead of the forest fire. Ponzie came running to greet us at the door.

"Thunder! Look, Thunder! Ciara's mom found my parents!" she yipped excitedly. "After the fire, she took me to the vet to see if I was chipped, and I am! I totally forgot I had a chip. Now my mom and dad are here to take us home—and with the new baby too! Come see, Thunder!"

Ponzie's dad gave me a pat on the head, and her mom held up the new baby for me to sniff. Pee-ew! There was no mistaking that diaper factor, but of course, in this case, I kept that to myself and said politely, "That's the cutest human baby I've ever seen. It's almost as cute as your dachshund puppies." Ponzie beamed with pride.

When it was time to leave, the couple buckled the baby into an extra-sturdy-looking car seat. Then they tucked the puppies into a car kennel with the words "Heavy Duty Crash Tested" printed on the top.

"Thank you both for everything," Ponzie smiled, "and please pass my thanks along to Spot and your friends. I'm so happy to be going home!" Her dad boosted her into the kennel, and the car started down the driveway. "Bye! See you around the park!" Ponzie barked.

"Snuggle those puppies for me!" Ciara barked.

"Goodbye!" I barked, smiling. Seeing Ponzie so happy to go home to her family made me feel happy too.

"You're right. That's what really matters," I said to Ciara, indicating the car with the happy family now all together again. "I don't care about the headline or my picture in the newspaper. I like to be helpful. That's why I'm a junior park ranger."

"I know," Ciara said. She leaned against me as we sat watching the car drive away. Then she said, "Come on, Thunder. Race you to Little Long Pond!" and we were off.

50036554R00108

Made in the USA
Middletown, DE
27 June 2019